2/21

ANGEL OF GREENWOOD

ANGEL of GREENWOOD

RANDI PINK

FEIWEL AND FRIENDS
New York

The author is grateful to the Tulsa Historical Society for providing primary source material about Greenwood and the Tulsa Race Massacre, and also to Mr. Hannibal B. Johnson, Esq., chair of the Education Committee for the 1921 Tulsa Race Massacre Centennial Commission, for his expert review of the material contained herein.

A FEIWEL AND FRIENDS BOOK
An imprint of Macmillan Publishing Group, LLC
120 Broadway, New York, NY 10271
fiercereads.com

Our books may be purchased in bulk for promotional, educational, or business use. Please contact your local bookseller or the Macmillan Corporate and Premium Sales Department at (800) 221-7945 ext. 5442 or by email at MacmillanSpecialMarkets@macmillan.com.

Library of Congress Cataloging-in-Publication Data is available.
First edition, 2021
Book design by Michelle Gengaro-Kokmen
Feiwel and Friends logo designed by Filomena Tuosto
Printed in the United States of America

ISBN 978-1-250-76847-6 (hardcover)

1 3 5 7 9 10 8 6 4 2

THE MOST POWERFUL OF THE SCRIBES
IS THE ONE WITHOUT FEAR.
IT'S WHAT I ASPIRE TO BE.

—MARY ELIZABETH JONES PARRISH,
FEARLESS AUTHOR OF *EVENTS OF THE TULSA DISASTER*
(1922; NOW OUT OF PRINT)
I HONOR YOU.

ANGEL

Everything was as it should be on the nineteenth day of May in the hopeful year of 1921. A slight tornado risk teased Greenwood Avenue with warm easterly winds and dirt in the eyes; still, the streets were buzzing. The only sounds filling the air on Angel Hill's side of the district were fluttering birds and grinning children off in the quaint distance.

Angel's father motioned for her to sit next to him on their front porch swing. When she reached, he grabbed both of her cheeks and stared so deep into her eyes that she saw her own reflection staring back through his own. Oklahoma heat drew beads of sweat from his pores, and he looked so tired to Angel; still, for his sake, she forced herself to smile.

"Mercy and truth," he said as he balanced his lemonade between his frail knees. "No such thing as mercy without

1

truth or truth without mercy. God granted them both to us all. And they work together like a bird on a breeze. What on earth does that mean to you, Angel, my love?"

"I do wonder," Angel replied. "Mercy is to take pity, while truth is a reliable thing. One is a feeling, an emotion untouchable, and the other is concrete veracity. But then, you can't forgive people without being honest, so maybe truth is in itself forgiveness. How then, Papa, could they work together to create anything?"

"Don't you see?" he said with small tears making the corners of his weak eyes twinkle. "It's the fight. Even the bird on the breeze is in perpetual battle with the winds. She makes it look easy. It is not easy. She makes it look enjoyable. It is not. Ah, look at her and tell me what you think she longs for."

He pointed to the orange-faced swift riding thin air. Her closed beak directing the remainder of her tiny body to glide and pump, glide and pump, glide and pump, and, finally, to glide into the thick of a soapberry tree.

"She wants . . . ," Angel said. "Rest."

"Just so," he said softly. "Rest within unrest. It is impossible."

When Angel looked back at her father, he was crying for the third time she'd seen in her sixteen years living. Angel honed in on his trembling chin, dimpled and pulled into the most heartrending frown. "Why do you cry, Papa?"

She lifted her thumb to catch his tears before they dropped.

After a few moments, he spoke. "My fight is nearly done, Angel, my love," he said with a bouncing, quivering grin.

"Yours is beginning, and for that, I am sorry. I wish for you mercy. I pray for you truth. I long for you the peace of sitting on a porch swing beside a man who loves you more than life itself. But I sense trouble on those winds. We've been dodging it for a time just like the swift in the soapberry. It's coming, dear child. I'd swear it is."

New shadows formed on his face, underneath his eyes, over his brow, and even in the crease of his hunched shoulders. He himself seemed to be becoming a shadow. Quick sketches of what he used to be a few short months ago. Angel knew him. And even in the quiet spaces, she saw flashes in his eyes. In those moments, she read what he was thinking—*to be reduced to this.*

Soft snores accompanied the rise and fall of his chest. He slept so easily now. One moment awake, and the next, dead to the world.

"I've got a gift for you. It'll be finished tomorrow," she whispered into his sleeping ear. "You'll walk again, sweet Papa. All on your own, you will."

Angel's mother pushed through the screen door as she untied her half apron. "We need to get him to bed," she said, trying so very hard to be strong. "You ready?"

"Yes, ma'am," Angel replied before lifting her father's limp arm around the nape of her neck.

"Time for bed," her mother said in the height of the afternoon sun. She then lifted the opposite arm around her own tired shoulder. "Handsome man of mine. One, two, three . . ."

ISAIAH

Most of Greenwood would be at Friday-evening Bible study at Mount Zion, so Isaiah Wilson's side of the district was quiet. He sat legs crossed on the sill of his bedroom window, reading. Ever since his father had fallen in the big war, Isaiah had been reading and writing voraciously. This time, he'd chosen poetry to bring him a sense of calm. The methodical, steady rhythms and occasional rhymes occupied his otherwise-frustrated mind. Lately, he'd been trying his hand at writing it. He wasn't that bad, either, if he said so himself. Then in the corner of his eye, he caught sight of them for the second time this week.

"White boys," Isaiah said aloud in his dark bedroom. "Damn white boys."

Isaiah had the perfect, bird's-eye view as they gathered on

the other side of the Frisco tracks. The pack was growing; last week there were twelve of them, and today, sixteen. They looked to be around his age, seventeen, and they were up to something, that much was for sure.

The Klan had been stirring around Tulsa lately. They'd been on an upswing since the war ended. And these boys either already were or were about to be wearing the white hats.

That's when he saw Angel Hill, a girl who lived a few streets over, off in the distance, walking alone. Isaiah's stomach turned because she couldn't know the group of white boys was there.

With Greenwood quiet, Angel would be ambushed, no question. And even from the distance, Isaiah could tell the boys were itching for mischief. Still, he was frozen with a fear he'd never felt before. And also, a question—should he intervene?

Tall but waif thin and hardly a commanding presence, Angel made her way up the street, still oblivious. Grasping hold of a contraption that looked like leg braces or walk assists, and wearing a long church dress and deftly pointing her toes as she walked in the near night. She was the perfect target.

From his perch, Isaiah saw the moment the boys spotted her. The small group ducked behind a thicket and waited for her to step within striking distance, like snakes in high grass. Isaiah didn't mean to, but he ducked, too, behind the tail of his bedroom curtain so they wouldn't see him. He knew that his father would be disappointed by his cowardice, but something within him couldn't get involved.

Besides, Isaiah didn't even know Angel Hill. Well, he knew her as well as anyone from Greenwood knew anyone else from Greenwood. Actually, if he were being honest with himself, he did know her.

Isaiah had seen her dance once before in a talent show. He recalled being envious of her, because she was wholly herself, answering to absolutely no one.

Isaiah remembered her walking barefoot to the center of the stage. He remembered waiting for a pianist or violinist or someone to join her there, but no one did. There was only her, alone in haunting silence.

The audience laughed at her awkward, twitchy movements, and Isaiah knew that they didn't understand. But in the silence, he understood. What confidence that took. What strength. To stand alone with no accompaniment and move her body as if freeing it from its chains. Isaiah saw her that day. As everyone made fun of her for being herself, Isaiah secretly saw her. He looked away, pretending that he didn't, but dear God he saw her.

Now hidden in the curtain, Isaiah told himself that he surely didn't know her well enough to go down there. He pulled the fabric around tighter until only his right eye would be showing from the outside. She'd be fine without his help. She would run.

"Run," he whispered into the curtain. "Now."

She'd run away, he thought. Of course she would. Anyone would.

But when the boys rose from behind the brush, Angel did not run. Instead, she stood tall, revealing her whole height to the unworthy troupe. She rose like she had on the stage of that talent show. Isaiah wished that he could snap a photograph or write a poem. The contrast between them was stark. Powerful in a way he'd never seen before. She nearly glowed; it was a wonder those white boys weren't shielding their eyes.

They spoke to her. Some circling like dirty birds on a scent, a few sniggering, and the rest hanging back. Cowards. He couldn't hear what they were saying, so he gently placed both hands on the sill and lifted the window.

The noise rang out much louder than Isaiah had expected, and every one of them looked—all sixteen white boys and Angel Hill, too. He curled himself deeper in the curtain and hoped they hadn't seen him. Maybe they hadn't, since they quickly turned their attention back to Angel.

"What you got there, gal?"

"Something worth something, I'd bet."

"Sure looks it!"

"Well," she replied slowly and deliberately, without an ounce of obvious fear on her words. "I'm not sure that's any of your business."

"Oh, you've got some nerve."

They closed in on her statuesque frame, and something flipped inside of Isaiah. He couldn't stand there, hiding in the curtain, while Angel Hill was ensnared by such filth. He parted his lips to yell out, but before he could holler at them, she dropped her contraption and ran into the night.

The thugs laughed and began inspecting the fallen equipment. Then, suddenly, the skinniest boy Isaiah had ever seen lifted the crutches and slammed them to the ground as hard as he could. The boy cursed the fact that even his most powerful whack left only a small scratch on them.

The other fifteen boys chuckled at him, and that's when the skinny boy lost himself in a fit of rage. He began pounding the crutches onto the rim of the Frisco tracks with as much force as he could muster. After a few minutes, they were shattered.

"Yeah!" he yelled in the direction Angel Hill had run. "How do you like that?"

Isaiah watched them backing away from the Greenwood District, kicking up dust and rocks as they walked. Something sinister was in the air, Isaiah could feel it. Something was coming.

ANGEL

A ngel's father still slept as she and her mother prepped the kitchen for the Barney sisters' arrival. While laying bright pink bows and barrettes across the cleared kitchen table, Angel saw the boy in her mind, lifting her father's crutches high and slamming them down for no reason at all. He was the angriest boy she'd ever seen. Angrier than anyone should dare be with life in his lungs.

It hadn't even been twelve hours since she'd watched the group of boys smash the crutches on the tracks. She'd saved up a month of helping her mother braid hair to afford them, and then spent another three weeks tinkering and repairing to make them perfect for her father.

Such a proud man, her father was. Before illness hit him, he reveled in the vigor of being born strong. When she was a small child, he'd throw her so far up into the air that she thought she was flying. Her mother would smack him on his purposely flexed upper arm, and he'd smack her right back on the rear end. Angel remembered covering her eyes for that, but what joy it brought her to witness such a love in her own home.

Then, like a slap, sickness made his strong body weak. He'd been in denial for a long time. Pushing away help and continuing to work as if he wasn't unwell. Then, one day after church, he fell hard on the front stoop and bled more blood than Angel could imagine being inside of a body. After that, the decline was swift. He managed to keep his spirits up, right until he wasn't able to walk on his own. After that, his smile never quite reached his eyes.

Angel had hoped those crutches would bring her father's smile back. But the unhappy, skinny boy had smashed that hope in less than three minutes. Angel felt a tremble come over her.

"Baby?" her mother said before grabbing Angel's shivering hands to her bosom. "What in the world are you thinking? You look like a fair ghost."

Angel hadn't said anything to her mother about the crutches. They were to be a gift to her, too. To see her beloved husband walk again would mean as much to her as it would have to him. Angel forced a grin onto her face.

"It's nothing, Mama," she said. "Dreading those Barney sisters is all."

Her mother released her hands and shook her head in agreement. "Yes, goodness," she replied. "Those are some hollering girls. I would send you along, but please, baby, I can't handle them without you. How about I raise your money up? I'll give you a ten cents instead of five. How's that sound?" A thin smile floated on the surface of her mother's tired expression. "Sounds good, Mama," Angel replied, wondering if her mother could see through her, too.

It really did sound good, though. Maybe it would only take Angel a couple of weeks to save up for new crutches.

Suddenly, the three Barney sisters banged hard on the back-door screen and ran in like the kitchen was a playground. Something inside of Angel came alive when children were around. An ability to relate to them on their level in ways that adults could not. That's why her mother couldn't handle them without assistance. Angel was not great at braiding their hair, but she was wonderful at making them sit calmly.

"Sit yourselves down, girls!" Her mother yelled at a volume that accomplished nothing. "Right now! Sit! Sit! Sit! Lord have mercy, Jesus! Sit! Sit! Sit!"

"Mercy," Angel said simply, and then she turned to the three sisters. "All right, girls. Ready for your surprise?"

They replied with a chorus of yeses so sweet that even Angel's mother tilted her head and beamed at them cautiously.

"This week . . . ," Angel said, reaching for the basket atop the high kitchen pantry, "a puppet show!"

The three young Barney sisters bounced on their heels

and rubbed their hands together like there was nothing on earth better than hand-sewn puppets made of remnant cloth.

"Gimmee! Gimmee! Gimmee!" they said.

"You'll have to sit in your seats, real, real quiet, each of you," Angel told them coolly. "And only after you're all done getting your hair braided." Angel replaced the puppets in the out-of-reach basket. "Then they've got a snazzy show to put on, especially for you three. Agreed?"

The sisters scurried to their seats and waited quietly for their hair to be greased, parted, and braided. Angel's mother stood in awe and watched her daughter work.

"Mama?" Angel said to her adoring mother. "It's showtime."

ISAIAH

Children crossed busy intersections in dresses and bow ties, followed closely by proud, dapper fathers balancing unlit cigars between their grinning teeth. Hatted and gloved mothers led the charge, holding up their frilly pocketbooks to halt postured men on horseback as if daring them to run over their sweet families. Streetcars hissed as the Barney sisters frolicked up and down the sidewalks, showing off their fresh hairdos. All shops, barber to blacksmith, had closed for the Sabbath and everything was just so. Everything, that is, except seventeen-year-old Isaiah Wilson, sitting on the frontmost pew of Sunday school at Mount Zion Baptist.

While he was always in attendance for regular services, he considered two-and-a-half-hour Sunday school a bore. After much argument, his mother had finally hauled him there, and he definitely regretted it. Isaiah lazily kicked dimples into the thick maroon carpet as the first lady of the church read aloud the sick and shut-in list. He flipped through the red-and-gold hymnal, searching for a song he cared to learn the words to, but the only ones he recognized were "Amazing Grace" and "Holy, Holy, Holy!"

He should've brought his well-worn copy of *The Souls of Black Folk*, by his favorite author, W.E.B. Du Bois, but he'd left it underneath his pillow from the night before. Isaiah had all but memorized the work in its entirety, but still he kept rereading, chasing the exhilaration he'd felt the very first time.

Back then, he'd been eleven years old, gripped by Booker T. Washington's philosophies. Greenwood's public high school donned his name—Booker T. Washington High School—and Isaiah wanted to fit in by the time he reached those grades. He sought out Washington's words and devoured them for many years. He was trapped in that familiar space of nothing-can-be-better-than-Booker, when Mrs. Edith, Greenwood District's lead librarian, handed him *The Souls of Black Folk* and he was immediately set free.

Du Bois spoke to Isaiah's longing for an active role in the future of his people. Like Du Bois, he was tired of waiting for someone else to save him. Tired of pretending proper in front of ravenous white folks while they drained his community of its hard work and culture. Tired of waiting and watching like he had a few nights prior from behind that pitiful curtain. And tired, most of all, of anticipating the next attack. Everyone knew it was coming, sooner or later, maybe even to a community as idyllic as Greenwood. Isaiah could feel it deep in his bones, and he knew that he was strong enough to meet it head-on. Brilliant enough. Brave enough. Talented enough to save himself and his people. Du Bois's book was a masterpiece, putting to words Isaiah's youth and Blackness in ways Washington hadn't.

Isaiah took a dull pencil from his suit jacket and began transcribing his favorite passages directly from memory to pass slow church time.

> With other black boys the strife was not so
> fiercely sunny: their youth shrunk into tasteless
> sycophancy, or into silent hatred of the pale
> world about them and mocking distrust of
> everything white; or wasted itself in a bitter
> cry, Why did God make me an outcast and a
> stranger in mine own house?

As imagination of him walking alongside W.E.B. Du Bois swept his mind away from Sunday school, he felt a twisting pinch to his rib cage.

"Ouch!" he yelled out, calling attention to him and his mother, who was silently apologizing to surrounding church members. "That one hurt!"

With a stealthy movement, his mother snatched the squatty pencil from his grasp. She must've peeked over his shoulders to read the passage as he was daydreaming.

"Stop writing that militant nonsense," she told him in a whisper. "It's counterintuitive to our cause."

She was onto him, he thought, also she was wholly wrong—stuck in her docile ways in a world that demanded action and movement. This was the mentality that had kept him frozen behind the curtain while Angel Hill stood threatened. Regret entered his tense body as he realized the magnitude of his own cowardice. Du Bois never would've hidden. He would have burst through the door, revealing himself a savior. Isaiah sat in his regret until it passed, and then, with nothing left to write with, he folded his arms and simmered.

Greenwood folks filled the church with an orchard of flowered hats and fedoras. A symphony of fluttering fans stapled sturdily onto Popsicle sticks brought the wind, while Pastor's sermon brought the fire, blazing the congregation into singular accord. Isaiah wished he could do this one day—meld a people into one body, shifting back and forth together without ever realizing. But he couldn't even convince his mother to love Du Bois as much as he did. And worse, he couldn't convince himself to be brave.

By the end of Sunday school, the pastor opened the floor for weekly testimonies. Seventy-eight-year-old Mother Williams, as always, went first. Shakily thanking God for being here today and waking her up this morning and such. Hypercompetitive and never to be outdone, eighty-year-old Mother Jackson went second. Equally shakily thanking God for being here today, and yes, waking her up this morning. She won that round with an impromptu rendition of "A Charge to Keep I Have." Then went everyone else—a procession of similar thankfulness and praise hands. After the thirteenth, Isaiah was having trouble with his heavy eyelids. In addition to the redundant testimonies, the Oklahoma heat was draining him of energy and thoughts.

"Wake up, child!" his mother said with an elbow to his still-aching ribs. "You're in the Lord's house."

By the time the choir marched in for 10:45 A.M. service, they'd already been there two whole hours. He kept huffing at his mother's lavender lace hat and her praise hands raised toward the wooden cross hanging from the ceiling and the painting of pale blue-eyed Jesus centered on the rear wall directly behind it. Even more dread took him over when the male chorus marched in with a depressed, synchronized sway. The male chorus was never music; it was instead a low, guttural growl and a moan, entirely without harmony or exuberance. Just his luck, he thought, he'd chosen to go to Sunday school on the male chorus's Sunday to lament.

As the gloomy choir rocked side to side grumbling "This Little Light of Mine," Isaiah thought, never again would he accompany his mother to pre-church. There were so many things he could be doing with his time rather than listening to what sounded like baritone birds dying in unison. He could be walking around Greenwood with his best friend, Muggy, whose family owned the town butcher shop. Or he could simply be sitting on his porch and writing his poetry or reading some

17

of his favorite works. He knew he shouldn't have given in to his mother. He folded his lean arms even tighter.

"All heads bowed," said the pastor after the male chorus finally took their seats in the stand behind him. "All eyes closed."

After prayer, Mother Evans began singing the Lord's Prayer a cappella from the pulpit, and three young girls dressed in ankle-length white dance robes pushed each other out of the rear study and onto their makeshift dance floor. The congregation chuckled at the youngest one, who kept stepping on her robes and stumbling, but the last one out brought all laughter to a quick halt.

It was Angel Hill.

The stark white silk against her deep dark complexion made Isaiah feel like he was trying to stare at the sun. His eyes unconsciously began to squint, and he quickly shook it off. Someone might have been watching him, but after a quick look around the sanctuary, he knew that no one was. On that strangely hot, tornadic, spring Sunday morning, the only thing anybody in that room saw was Angel.

Without inhibition, she danced. With passionate expression and force, pressing against something that needed to be defied. She threw around her toned arms and fought the air with closed fists. On the tips of her toes, she spun around so fast he thought she might knee the rim of the baptizing pool, but she didn't. She was both power and serenity. Skill and rawness. Activism and patience. When she reached the center, the younger two girls fell to their knees around her to give her the spotlight she deserved.

To Isaiah, she was the girl who had faced those boys. Anyone else would have bolted immediately, Isaiah knew. But even when he whispered it into the curtain, the girl stood. Face-to-face with an evil so loveless. And then mere days later, she was able to find enough love within herself to spin a congregation fond. She was captivating. He'd seen her in a glimpse that day at the talent show, but he could press that down deep and deny it.

This? Only feet in front of him, he could not ignore a magic such as this.

Angel's solo lasted for the entire second half of the song, but Isaiah could no longer hear Mother Evans's singing. There was only Angel, spinning Greenwood's thirty-five blocks into something much more confusing and complicated. He was a man of seventeen, best friend to Muggy Little Jr.: the self-crowned love king of Greenwood Avenue. He was an aspiring foot soldier in the swelling ground war of societal change led by the one and only W.E.B. Du Bois. And since his father died a few years ago in the big war, most important, Isaiah was the man of the house.

A real man wouldn't notice Angel's hair was wild and free and more beautiful than anything he'd ever seen in his life. A real man wouldn't wonder if she liked Du Bois as much as he did or if she cared for activism at all. A real man didn't watch the most peculiar girl in school dance as if she were some kind of an angel. And a real man certainly didn't feel unworthy of watching her dance in front of him like she was living, breathing, moving poetry.

He forced his gaze back to the maroon carpet until the song had ended. When it did, everyone, even the elderly mothers of the church, stood to their feet. Some outright cried afterward, and others pretended not to. He stood along with them so he wouldn't look odd, but didn't dare look up at her. Real men surely didn't cry.

ANGEL

On the second-to-last day of school, Angel sat on the front stoop of her house, hugging five large books to her chest and humming the Lord's Prayer. As usual, she was ready early, so she tucked her knees inside of her long navy skirt and listened to the crisscrossing groups of chirping birds perched atop her favorite weeping soapberry tree. Suddenly, the sound of her neighbor Mrs. Nichelle's screaming infant punctured the peace of her quiet street.

Everyone else was sleeping or already off to work and school, including Mrs. Nichelle's husband, the high school vice principal, Mr. Anniston. Angel's heart went out to her neighbor, left alone with their colicky six-month-old baby boy, Michael. Peeking at her ticking pocket watch, Angel saw that she had twenty more minutes before she should set off for the schoolhouse. She jumped to her feet and went over to knock on her neighbor's screen door.

"Who's there?" Mrs. Nichelle asked frantically over Michael's screams.

"It's me. Angel. Anything I can help with? I'm a bit early again."

"You're a godsend," Mrs. Nichelle said as she pushed through the screen door with Michael dangling from her hip. He was bright red from his yelling and as mad as a viper. "Few moments of privacy would do me good. I've been holding it all night."

"Of course," said Angel. She held her hands out for Michael to fall into them. Mrs. Nichelle squeezed her legs together, and she quickly walked toward the bathroom. "Take as long as you need."

Angel rocked Michael on her neighbor's front step for what felt like a while, and she glanced at her ticking watch to see that an hour had passed. Angel's first mind told her to go check on Mrs. Nichelle, but Michael had finally dozed off on her upper shoulder. She decided to let him sleep. But then a second hour had passed. He was snoring, blowing tiny spit bubbles while he slept. Angel didn't dare put him in his crib; he'd surely wake up raging.

Angel found peace in the simplicity of rocking a neighbor's fussy baby to sleep and watching the smaller birds chase the larger ones away from their nests hidden in the soapberry. She thought of what her father had told her of the birds in that very tree. He'd said they were longing for rest within unrest. While gently rocking Michael, she thought, that's all any of us long for really. Especially Black folks in these shifty times. So many had crossed the Frisco tracks in search of rest, and in Greenwood, they'd found it.

When sweat began dripping from the tiny tip of Michael's nose, she headed toward the Williamses' drugstore for a cold drink and cool air. As she walked, the sun scrambled in the approaching clouds, trying greatly to get a peek at the gorgeous Greenwood District. It was another one of those days just like the day before, phony storm telling people to stay indoors. But Angel knew there was nothing behind it—only the bluster of trickster gray clouds. Still, with tiny Michael resting on her now-aching shoulder, rolling sky two days in a row sent tiny chills up her back. Her papa had told her that God'll send signs to the most observant among us. Most ignore them with blind, unreasonable faith. But the chosen few moved through life according to those signals, like a chimney train on its tracks, he'd say.

The pungent aroma of man-tall juniper lined the walkways alongside her quiet street, effectively taking attention from the ominous above. Mrs. Tate's blue house on the corner was the origin of the smell. Her juniper won prizes all over. She'd nursed it through the driest Oklahoma droughts and even the fluke cold spell a few years back. Her husband owned and ran the Greenwood pharmacy, and when her only son, Timothy, went south for medical school, she'd shifted her mothering to the juniper. And Angel's already-manicured street benefitted greatly. Mrs. Tate, however, was never nearly as pleasant as her juniper.

When Mrs. Tate peeked over a cone-shaped shrub taller than she was, Angel leaped back with her hand firmly on Michael's rear end. She was a tiny woman, flitting around like a hummingbird. She wore wide-brimmed hats to keep the sun at bay and zip-front flowered housedresses.

"Just me, Angel," Mrs. Tate called out in a whisper. "Nice of you to watch Nichelle's boy. He's a hollerer, that one."

Feeling defensive of Michael, Angel ignored the slight affront and instead focused on the two things Mrs. Tate cared for in the world. "Your juniper is looking better than I've ever seen it. Oh, and how's Timothy?"

As expected, Mrs. Tate's face lit up with gladness. "Tim's a dream of a son. An absolute dream. His letter came today, you know that? Handwriting of a champion. Always knew he'd grow up to be something special. He was a good baby. No hollering and carrying on like that one there you're holding on to."

"We should really get on our way," Angel interrupted as respectfully as possible. "Little man's sweating in his sleep. We're heading on to the Williamses' shop for a sip." Angel began walking. "See you later on."

"Come on back by soon!" Mrs. Tate reluctantly waved. "So I can finish up telling you about my boy. And this juniper, too!"

By the end, Mrs. Tate was yelling her words. Angel made a mental note to take the long way home.

ISAIAH

There was no room left in Isaiah's mind—only Angel.

But this was not the fate of the Black boys of 1921. This was for daydreamers who walked through life tripping over their own loafers. This was for woolgatherers, aimlessly grinning at nothing. This, most of all, was for white boys.

White boys could get away with an all-consuming kind of love. They could learn every meticulous baritone note within "Let Me Call You Sweetheart," gather a quartet, and serenade their loves with no consequences to follow. No impending smack at the nape of the neck from steely fathers or philandering best friends. With no worry of looming revolution or invasion, they got to fall in love. And love, after all, was the only thing in the world that mattered. Love could lead a man to long for much more than mediocrity. Love of family. Love of community. It was a force stronger than hate, Isaiah realized. It was also, for him, not allowed.

And then there he was. Walking to school, surrounded by the excellence of the formerly enslaved—the very demonstration of that type of powerful, perseverant love. Those who pulled themselves up to build and create and manufacture for the sake of community and family. Yet still, Isaiah toiled internally from the wrongness of the *us* and *them*. Envying a simplicity existing a mere stone's throw over the Frisco railroad tracks. Isaiah was not one man, but two—himself and his black shadow—following him, sometimes pestering him, to utilize his own ingenuity in order to navigate the world made complicated by the color of his skin.

Through the concept of double consciousness, Du Bois had said as much in *Souls*:

> *It is a peculiar sensation, this double-*
> *consciousness, this sense of always looking at*
> *one's self through the eyes of others, of measuring*
> *one's soul by the tape of a world that looks on*
> *in amused contempt and pity. One ever feels his*
> *twoness,—an American, a Negro; two souls,*
> *two thoughts, two unreconciled strivings; two*
> *warring ideals in one dark body, whose dogged*
> *strength alone keeps it from being torn asunder.*

A sharp slap at his nape snapped Isaiah back to the mundane reality of walking to school with his best friend, Muggy Little Jr.

"Get your dreamy head out the clouds," Muggy told him, twisting his unlit cigar between thumb and index finger. "Have you heard a word I've said?"

Isaiah shrugged in return. "I believe you were talking about . . . Frances."

"That was last week," Muggy said, very proud of himself. "Try again."

"Helen?"

"Two months ago." Muggy laughed. "Again."

"Okay, Gladys."

Muggy doubled over in hysterics. "Am I really this much of a dog?"

"Just tell me," Isaiah replied. "And no, I wasn't listening."

"Dorothy Mae," Muggy said before twisting a spin in the middle of the street. "Foxy broad. And more than willing, if you know what I mean?"

"I do," Isaiah replied. He'd been necking around with Dorothy Mae for many months now. Beautiful she was, but not much for conversation.

"Oh, yeah." Muggy chuckled. "You and Dorothy had a little something, you mind if I . . ."

Again, Isaiah shrugged and walked ahead.

This was what was expected of Black boys like him, Isaiah thought. He was to be a Muggy, uselessly spreading himself around like the whites of a dandelion on the wind. What was he to dare do? Challenge Muggy? Never. If he did, there would be hell to pay.

Muggy's family butcher business was booming. Even white folks crossed the tracks to get their hands on his father's cuts. The Littles had more than they needed, and after Isaiah's father fell in the war, they'd agreed to pass along some of their extra to Isaiah's mother. Most of the district did. From the neighborhood pharmacist to the growers, Greenwood chipped in to help prop up Isaiah's household. He, therefore, was quietly indebted to them all, even his best friend. Isaiah could never show himself as he truly was on the inside. He could only acquiesce and get through the day.

"She's a fine dame," Isaiah said of Dorothy Mae, still walking ahead so Muggy couldn't read his face. "But not mine alone to have. Do with her what you will."

Isaiah hung his head slightly, and Muggy leaped into the air and onto Isaiah's back, nearly pulling them both to the ground. "Attaboy!" Muggy hollered. "What were you daydreaming about anyway? Looks like your mind's lost in your own dame."

"Actually . . . ," Isaiah said, leaning sideways to ease Muggy, who was a head shorter than him, off of his back. "Have you heard much about double consciousness?"

Muggy let out an audible huff. "Not this Du Bois foolishness again," he replied. "Look around you!" Muggy held his arms open and spun around twice. "We're living in a Black man's paradise. We're free to come and go as we please, walk down our own streets, sipping our own cola and smacking our own broads on the backside."

"Yes," Isaiah replied, facing Muggy. "But for a Black man in a stranger's nation, are we ever truly safe? And too, whose nation even is this? Whose land are we walking on right now? Sure isn't theirs." Isaiah motioned toward the white side of Tulsa. "Look at this . . ." Isaiah lifted his well-worn copy of *Souls* from his innermost jacket pocket. And in response, Muggy dramatically plugged his ears.

"If you tell me one more thing Du Bois said in that damn book, I'll scream," Muggy snapped, and then grabbed Isaiah by the shoulders to stare him directly in the eyes. "Nothing ever happens in the Greenwood District. If revolution comes, it doesn't even need to come here. We're Black folks governing Black folks. Minding our own damn business, just like them." Muggy pointed across the Frisco tracks to a small group of white teenagers leaning against a soda machine. "Long as we keep to ourselves, we could live like this forever. Now tell me about the dame you're daydreaming about. No man looks at the sky like that if it isn't about a dame."

Isaiah peered over to the group Muggy had just pointed out. These were the same boys who'd broken Angel Hill's belongings. Minding their business, they were not. That much was so apparent, and Isaiah couldn't understand how Muggy didn't notice it, too.

ANGEL

With two blocks left to walk, Angel's upper arm was nearly numb from Michael's weight. Small but solid, he was beginning to feel like a stack of heavy books, and she longed to shift him to another shoulder. Also, his baby sweat shone through his tiny clothing and now began to saturate her school shirt. She quickened her steps; he needed cool.

With one and a half blocks remaining, she heard her name again. "Angel, Angel!" Mr. Morris called out from his porch swing across the sidewalk. Angel knew his voice without seeing him. He peeked over his own impressive garden, filled with blooming pink evening primrose and freshly popped basket flower. Mr. Morris was one of her favorites of Greenwood. So very kind and patient, he'd recently retired, passing on his wood-carving shop to his eldest son, George.

She waved to him with her free hand and smiled. "We'll stop back by another time," she said. Mr. Morris nodded along, but she wasn't sure he'd actually heard. Decades of close-up work with machinery had taken with it the majority of his hearing.

He wore blue overalls and a newsboy cap, and he smiled with all his teeth. "See you when I see you, little lady!"

Angel was beginning to realize a quick stroll through Greenwood might not be feasible. Everybody knew everybody, and Angel with sleeping Michael on her shoulder, on a school day no less, was fair reason for investigation. She quickened her steps even more. Past the manicured lawns, budding flower beds, and monstrous magnolia trees shading bits of sidewalk; then she finally reached Deep Greenwood, the business district.

Relieved to see the rim of town, she slowed her stroll to take in the red-and-brown brick buildings along the busy strip. The finest of restaurants, clothiers, grocers, hardware shops—all owned by families she knew. Walkways filled by tailored men with dainty ladies holding on to their right elbows. Black, brilliant, self-sustaining Greenwood Avenue was proof that Booker T. Washington was correct about tolerance and eventual progress. He'd called it "Negro Main Street," which was in all ways apropos. Greenwood's success always brought to mind a famed quote of Washington's:

Success always leaves footprints.

Angel saw Washington's wisdom throughout Greenwood.

She also saw it in the railroad tracks, dividing white Tulsa from Black Greenwood. Those tracks were ever present in the consciousness of those on both sides. Unfair, of this there was zero doubt, but Washington gave permission to thrive alongside in segregation. And booming Greenwood proved him correct, rest his soul.

Michael burst awake as they entered the crowded drugstore and soda shop. An interested procession of questions greeted Angel, but now she didn't mind at all.

"Why aren't you at school, Angel?"

"Mrs. Nichelle's really been catching it with this sweet baby boy, hasn't she?"

"Did God send you straight from heaven, child? You truly live up to your name. Cokes on the house." Mrs. Williams had placed an ice-cold cola in Angel's free hand, and Michael was happy, cooing in the coolness of the storefront.

When Dr. Owens walked in the door, Angel immediately felt tension in her low gut. He was one of the only residents in the district who knew the extent of her father's condition, and she in no way wanted to discuss it. Greeted by soda-shop patrons at every step, he slowly made his way toward her table.

As Greenwood was concerned, Dr. Owens was as close to a famous person they had. A dapper man, always pressed and buttoned beneath his crisp lab coat. His unaffected smile never left his cheeks, making them plump, shiny, and youthful. He breezed through the town like a wide-winged bird. Unattached and without public conquests, he was the most desirable and classy of bachelors. Angel liked him enough, but since her father fell ill, all of his likability melted away. Now he was only the bearer of bad news.

"May I sit?" he asked her.

"You may," Angel replied, trying hard to give the impression that she most certainly did not want him to sit without being overly rude.

He pulled up a seat and spread his infectious grin ever further across his face. "How do you get him so calm?" he asked of Michael. "Every time he visits my office, the whole town can hear his cries. You've turned him into a reverie."

Angel stroked Michael's upper back with gentle, frustrated hands. "He's upset because he senses exactly this—the town's rebukes of him. We wouldn't speak so judgmentally of the temperaments of an adult; why does everyone feel so free to speak illy of a child? Let alone one also who cannot yet speak for himself. Anything could be bothering him. An itch he cannot reach, a sneeze he cannot release, a foul smell he cannot stand." She smiled and lifted him into the air. "He loves me because I dare give him grace."

After her speedy rant, Angel grasped the doctor's long silence and looked up at him to see concern on his usually jovial face.

"Angel," he started finally. "How are you holding up?"

This is exactly why she didn't want him to sit across from her that day. A wonderful doctor he was, that much was undeniable, but he meddled too much in feelings and emotions he knew nothing about.

"I'm perfectly fine, thank you," she replied stiffly. "Why do you ask?"

"Your father . . ."

"Anything else I can get you?" Mrs. Williams said only to Dr. Owens, forgetting completely that Angel was sitting there.

"No, thank you, ma'am," he replied to her, smile re-plastered on his face.

Without asking, Mrs. Williams pulled out the third seat and leaned in close to Dr. Owens. "My daughter is coming back from Spelman for the summer months," she said softly before peeking around to make sure no one else could hear. "She was first runner-up in the beauty contest this year. Did you know that?"

He grinned, but Angel could tell it was empty and rehearsed. "I think you've told me that a time or two, yes."

"She's mighty sought after, Doc."

"Yes, ma'am," he replied again. "You've told me that, too."

While they spoke, Angel slyly tightened her grip on Michael and guzzled the remainder of her Coke.

"Thanks for the drink, Mrs. Williams," she interjected, but Mrs. Williams waved her away. "See you soon, Dr. Owens."

Dr. Owens attempted to stand, but Angel held her hand out to stop him from doing so. "Next time," he started. "We need to have a real sit-down, sound good?"

Rudely, Angel didn't reply to that at all. Instead, she scurried out the door and toward home.

Angel took the long way and stayed close to the railroad tracks to avoid Mrs. Tate and, surprisingly, had run into no one. An extra-long passenger train passed, car after car after car. She always paused to revel in the beauty of trains, especially this kind—deep burgundy with opulent golden swirls. This train was mostly first-class and only available for whites, so she'd likely never tour the inside. This was as close as she could get, a timely peek here and a perfectly placed glance there. She could almost catch a glimpse of exquisite ladies in large, feathered hats walking the length of the cabins. In a particular light, she could see the dining car, her favorite, with smooth white tablecloths, laughing patrons, and stainless-steel towers of tiny biscuits in the center of each table.

Michael began to coo at the train, and Angel smiled. "I know, little man. It's mighty beautiful, isn't it?"

Again, he cooed and added a sweet smile along with it as the final box car rushed by them.

When she was small, her father had told her to always wave at the caboose of a train until it was completely out of sight. He'd told her it would bring her good fortune and the best of luck. For that reason, no matter what was happening, and no matter how foolish it made her look, she'd wave frantically at the backmost train car.

So she stood, feet planted, saying goodbye to the fleeting,

exclusive, out-of-reach train. Just like that, it was out of sight. Gone and on its way to a place not Greenwood.

After this, she went straight home to find out if Mrs. Nichelle had come looking for her.

"Hey, Papa," Angel said to her fragile father. "Mrs. Nichelle been by?"

"Not today," he replied with a labored smile. "Good thing she's married to the vice principal or else I might be worried about you playing hooky on the second-to-last day of school. Didn't you have a big Latin test this morning?"

"Like you said," Angel said. "Good thing this little guy's father is my vice principal. Besides, Mrs. Nichelle was really catching it this morning."

"I'm sure she's grateful," he said, wincing as he shifted himself on the couch.

"Anything I can bring you before I go back next door?"

"Just want to sit with my favorite girl for a while," he replied in broken breaths.

When he lifted his arm, he nearly tilted off the couch. Angel leaped to stop him from crashing onto the living room floor; she'd caught him in time, but Michael lunged on her hip and began to scream. He reached his tiny fingers for her father's cheek, and when Angel stopped him, he began wailing even more.

"Give him to me," said her father, who was hardly able to lift his own arm without flinching.

"You sure?" she asked. "You've been feverish lately."

"I think I can handle seventeen pounds pretty well," he said with a labored chuckle. "Come here, little man."

An unseen energy came over her father as the boy fell into his arms. Angel felt her heart break a little as she watched him bounce the baby on his tired, skinny knee. It must've been excruciating and exhausting to bounce like that, but her father did it with joy all over him. A similar joy came over Michael, too. He stopped flailing as soon as he sat with her father.

"See?" said her father. "He knows that I'm about to leave this place."

"Papa . . . ," Angel tried interrupting, but her father wouldn't allow it.

"Let me finish," he said calmly. "Children this age can tell who's coming and going soon. You ever notice that babies gravitate to expecting women? It's the same thing. They remember what we've forgotten."

"Papa," Angel started. "God's going to bring you out of this. I just know it."

Angel's father's breathing quickened. Then, after much thought, he said, "You know what? I agree with that with my whole heart."

Angel watched them, grinning at each other as if they were sharing a secret, and it hit her that she and her father were talking about two different types of deliverance. She meant healing, while he meant death.

She lifted Michael from her father's knee. "You need rest, Papa," she told him before walking back out the door.

"Did you see the sky today?" he asked her. "And yesterday, too?"

"I did see that," Angel replied.

Her father smiled, but it didn't reach his tired eyes, not even close. "A warning. Something's coming."

Angel watched his eyes slowly blink as if every one took away energy he didn't have to spare. "Rest now, Papa."

As she left her own dreary living room and looped her own backyard, Mrs. Nichelle ran outside to find her. "My God, Angel, I'm so sorry. I'd just closed my eyes for a minute, and I fell asleep by accident." She eased the baby from Angel and hugged her too tightly. "You're an angel, truly. I'll call Jack, I mean, Vice Principal Anniston, and let him know why you're so late."

"Anything you need, Mrs. Nichelle," Angel replied. "Now, I have to get to school before I miss it altogether."

"I can walk with you!"

"No, ma'am," she said, picking up her thick stack of books from her front porch. "Baby boy has been in the heat all day. He's worn out and calm. Enjoy the quiet while you can."

She jogged toward school with a wave.

Her high school was nearly a half mile away, but the walk was flat with new walkways and freshly popped purple verbena everywhere. The sunlight had been pulling them out for a while—all bright and warm—telling the underground bulbs that it was the ideal time to reveal their beautiful faces to the waiting world. They reminded her of another quote from her favorite orator, Booker T. Washington:

> *Success in life is founded upon attention to the*
> *small things rather than to the large things; to*
> *the everyday things nearest to us rather than to*
> *the things that are remote and uncommon.*

Washington spoke directly to her tender heart with such axioms. He packaged his activism in tolerance, a method highly superior to the likes of W.E.B. Du Bois, whose so-called action would only lead to more destruction. Washington, unlike Du Bois, was wise, patient, and calculating in his strategies of eventual change. Much like the sun teasing out verbena, Angel thought, Washington believed in the gentle power of waiting his turn. She was glad her high school donned his brilliant name.

She did, however, question. When she stood staring at burgundy boxcars with golden swirls that she could never see on the inside, she questioned. The blaring injustices and inequalities she'd learned about in history class, the stories and warnings from her father, the plight of her distant relatives. Angel was not naive; she certainly questioned. Never aloud, but on the quiet inside, doubt ran through her mind as quickly and as often as those fancy, untouchable trains ran along the Frisco tracks.

ISAIAH

"I can't right now," Isaiah whispered to Muggy. "I have a Latin test."

"It's Mrs. Greene," Muggy said as if Mrs. Greene weren't a real teacher who could give a real failing grade to both of them. "She's my father's best customer. We can throw a bit of extra bacon in her bag this Thursday or something. Come smoke with me. I've got to tell you about Dorothy Mae."

Nothing within Isaiah's body wanted to hear about Dorothy Mae or Frances or any other one of Muggy's conquests. Isaiah wanted only to take the Latin test. He'd studied hard for many days. He wanted to ace it as he knew he would, but in the same way Mrs. Greene would likely let Muggy slide, Isaiah couldn't say no to him, either. He hung his head and followed Muggy out to the back bleachers for a smoke.

Muggy slashed alive a matchstick before they even left the inside of the school and lit his fat cigar until it sizzled red at the tip. Puff, puff, puff, and then Muggy passed it to Isaiah.

"Here," Muggy said, smiling and proud. "Take a taste of that. My father brought it back from vacation last week. Well, what he calls vacation."

A hint of sadness flooded Muggy's usually overconfident countenance, so small only Isaiah could see it.

"All right?" Isaiah asked, not wanting to say too much. Muggy was a spitfire on edge whenever he brought up his father.

"All right," Muggy replied without seeming upset. "I know what everybody's saying about us. I'm not as stupid as you all act like I am."

"Muggy, I . . ."

"Know what my father told me when he got back this time?" Muggy asked as if Isaiah hadn't interjected. "He saw us walking together, me and you, and had the gall to tell me I should be a little more like you."

"I . . ."

"Isn't that just a hoot? Because when I was younger, he told me I should be like him. And you and him couldn't be more different." Muggy paused for a moment. "What is a son to do with such a father?"

After that, Isaiah knew better than to say anything else about it. Muggy's father was as successful a businessman as

Greenwood had to offer, but he was also a notorious double-dealer, with both his butcher business and his family.

He flaunted women freely throughout the district. Shamelessly embarrassing his demure wife and, Isaiah was now realizing, his son, too. While Muggy mostly spoke positively of his father, these rare moments of doubt were becoming more common and more apparent to Isaiah. Muggy was beginning to disapprove of his rogue father's fraud.

It was a strange position to be in, Isaiah thought. Wedged uncomfortably between an outwardly buoyant best friend's lifelong denials and a town's relentless gossip. Greenwood chattered about Muggy's father from as far back as Isaiah could recall. A crook, a shyster, fast-talking know-it-all, they'd called him. But above all, they labeled him a horrible husband, which was a source of irrevocable shame in Greenwood.

In the district, some men philandered, quietly stepping out on knowing wives in the dark of night, terrified of consequence. But Muggy Sr. was brazen. Uncompromisingly cheating. Grinning with all of his teeth as he grabbed ahold of a young, dainty willing hand while walking up and down Greenwood Ave. He relentlessly made his widely desired wife look both a fool of a woman and a victim to be rooted for. Isaiah long thought Muggy's father was the fool for not appreciating and respecting such a woman.

Muggy's mother stood up straight, and Isaiah couldn't recall a single wrinkle in her wardrobe, not one in the decade and a half he'd known her. She was easy to smile but never on his level. Her chin held a steady posture high in the air like a gazelle. And on the rare occasions when she was seen with her husband, she made him look like a shrimp of a man. Sad, short, and wider than he was tall. He wasn't on her level, either, and maybe he knew it. Maybe that was the point.

She'd taken the brunt of the Greenwood gossip since she dared to stand tall alongside a spouse so unworthy. But to look at her, no one would know she was affected. Isaiah recalled Muggy once justifying his father's public cheating as his mother's fault.

"If a man steps out," Muggy had long ago told Isaiah, "don't look at the man himself. Look instead at the man's wife. God punishes such a woman with eternal sadness and shame for not satisfying her husband."

Isaiah would never forget it because it was both shocking and pathetic in its callousness and disrespect. But now Isaiah wasn't sure Muggy still believed that. Now, it seemed, Muggy saw glimpses of his father in the same way Greenwood saw him—as a complete, irredeemable loser.

A shocking sizzle ran across Isaiah's forearm, making him jump into the air.

"What the hell was that?" Isaiah shouted.

Muggy laughed in response. "Oh, calm down. Just a glowing matchstick. Won't even leave a mark."

Isaiah held his slightly burned skin with his free hand and sat down next to Muggy. "Why would you do that?"

"I'm trying to figure out who you're daydreaming about," he said. "You don't just keep that kind of information from your best friend. Who is she?"

Isaiah shrugged. He knew that he couldn't be honest and tell him he was actually thinking of Muggy's mother and father. Their friendship was built on different things, shallower things. But Muggy was not entirely wrong.

Since yesterday, all of Isaiah's thoughts were shaded by Angel Hill. A deep brown hue of Angel, catching ahold of every light in her vicinity. Turning impossible turns. Generating heat in his icy heart, canceling out a quadrant of anger that he couldn't figure out how to rid himself of before he saw her dance. She was a Black magic he'd never witnessed, spinning the congregation around her pinkie in a matter of minutes.

Angel Hill, he would've said out loud to any other kind of best friend. Angel Hill, he might have divulged to a comrade more empathetic of the existence of a love like that. Angel Hill, he wanted to climb atop the empty bleachers and yell back at Muggy, but he wouldn't understand. A Black boy spun so tightly after magical dancing by a deep dark girl wearing ankle-length white? No one would.

ANGEL

Angel stopped in front of Deacon Yancey's light green house, bent forward, and took one long drag of the upright purple flower.

"Hello there," she said to the verbena. "You, my friend, have perfect posture. You should be a dancer."

When she stood back up again, Deacon Yancey was making his way onto his front porch holding a coffee mug.

He bowed to her as if she were royalty and said, "Your praise dance yesterday, Miss Angel, left the whole world a little bit better. Join me for a cup?"

Though it would only make her later for school, she nodded. "Of course, Deacon." He was lonely, after all. His wife of twenty-seven years had died the year prior.

She walked through his squatty white gate to find a hidden

field of more peeping verbena—red, pink, and a hybrid orangey swirl. The sight stopped her, and Deacon Yancey walked down to stand by her side.

"They're confused," he said before taking a small sip of steaming green tea. "Poor, sweet things don't realize my wife has passed on to glory. Have a seat on the swing, I'll bring you the best cup of honey tea you've ever had in your life."

As he disappeared into his small home, Angel breathed in crisp, hot air and watched the world from the vantage point of Deacon Yancey's front porch. His view of Greenwood was wholly different than the one from her own porch swing. For one, she could see the back field of her school from there. She squinted at two boys skipping class and hanging near the back of the wooden bleachers. It was Mother Wilson's son, Isaiah, and his friend Muggy Little Jr.

Being from such a small town, there was no avoiding others within it, but every time she caught herself about to pass Isaiah and Muggy in the halls, she purposely found an empty classroom nearby to detour. The few unfortunate times she'd run into them, they laughed at her for no reason at all.

Muggy especially was hard-boiled toward her. He'd called her ugly multiple times and even tried to trip her once when she wore a floor-length, long-sleeved, flowered dress to school. He'd pulled at her plaits throughout middle school and made her cry in elementary for too many reasons to name. He must've been born mean, she thought, because all she had to do was walk by him and his friends for them to double over in hysterics like her existence alone was enough to evoke laughter. But Isaiah was kinder. His nature clearly less abrasive. He simply didn't stand for anything. Isaiah went along to get along; that much was obvious to Angel, and she did not respect it.

Isaiah had come by Mount Zion for Sunday school the day before. She tilted her head. He'd even stood up after she danced, and clapped a little. Angel tried not to notice such things. Her praise dancing was for herself and the Lord, but there he was on the front row in an open ovation.

Angel watched as the cigar smoke rose from the bleachers. She tried to compare the Isaiah she'd always known to the one on the front row of church yesterday. It crossed her mind that maybe he was putting on for his friends. Maybe he wasn't a follower on the inside as he'd always seemed on the outside. But it surely wasn't her job to teach him how to stand up for what he believed.

Deacon Yancey excitedly burst through the screen door holding a Mount Zion mug filled to the brim with tea. "Take a sip of this here and tell me it isn't the best you've ever tasted."

Angel took a short sip and tried not to grimace. It tasted like gritty green dirt. Inside of the mug were tiny bits of sticks and leafy flakes; he'd pierced the tea bag, emptying the contents into the liquid. It was irrationally disgusting. Easily the most horrible cup of tea Angel had ever had.

"Mmm." She placed the cup on the small side table to her right. "I'll let it cool for a few moments, but mmm!"

"Yes, goodness," he said, still genuinely thrilled by his horrid cup of tea. "I think I just about have it perfect, like Mrs. Yancey used to." He looked off after mentioning his late wife.

Angel had noticed it every Sunday since she'd passed. He had no idea how to manage himself without his wife's help. Wrinkled, loose-necked shirts had replaced crisp, starched ones. He was scaly ankles, uncut hair, and bitter green tea now.

"How have you been getting along since?" Angel asked, not wanting, or having, to finish her unfinished sentence. He knew what she meant.

Worry came over his face—the look of a child lost in a boulevard. "Can't figure how one woman made so much happen in a day is all," he said, trying to smile but failing. "I didn't know just how much. I thought, like the fool I am, that a house fixed itself back every morning. In the same way I thought food came home delicious and kids went straight to sleep and shirts got crispy right out the wash. But sometimes, Angel girl, you just can't know how good you got it until it dies."

Angel thought about this before speaking. Death was dangerously close to her home, hovering over her living room like an angry cloud. If it swooped in today and took away her precious father, would she sit alone on a porch swing forever, regretting not appreciating him? Would it eat her up—those things unsaid, unthanked, unacknowledged?

The firm answer was no. She showed her appreciation to everyone around her, even those who didn't deserve it. She was a servant, put on this earth to help and love and caretake, just like Booker T. Washington was when he was alive. Deacon Yancey's fate was that of a man who didn't appreciate his wonderful wife until he lost her for good. Sad, heartbreaking, unfortunate, but not nearly Angel. She couldn't comfort him, she realized. Any response would be a lie. She shifted her gaze to the two boys in the practice fields and changed the subject.

"Deacon Yancey?" she asked while she swallowed the last stick in her green tea. "You seem to know everybody in this town. What do you know about Isaiah Wilson? He came by Sunday school yesterday."

Deacon Yancey let out a choking cough as if she'd asked about Satan himself. "Stay as far away from that boy as you can. I mean it."

"Yes, sir," she said, never daring question an elder.

She looked toward the bleachers again. Isaiah had walked closer to the fence and was staring directly at her. She caught his eye and quickly looked away. God had put her in this world to help people, not to stare back at mischievous follower Isaiah Wilson. She couldn't be bothered with a phony bad boy who skipped class and smoked expensive cigars by the bleachers with his rich friends. It was cliché at best—good girl saves bad boy from himself. No way.

Then she sneaked a second look to see that he was still staring, this time with his hand frozen in a wave. When she waved back, his friend Muggy smacked Isaiah's head from behind. Muggy didn't approve.

"Don't wave back, Angel. I forbid you. He's trouble with a capital T, that one," said Deacon Yancey, who didn't approve, either.

ISAIAH

"What was that?" Muggy said before taking a long drag from his second cigar. "Angel's been a bluenose since we were little."

"I can't wave at a girl?" Isaiah replied, snatching Muggy's cigar for a puff. "And she's not a bluenose. She's a dancer."

"A dancer?" Muggy frisked over to the fence to get a closer look.

"Don't stare." Isaiah covered his eyes with his hand. "Muggy, stop that right now, I mean it."

Turning toward Isaiah, Muggy asked, "How the hell else am I supposed to get a good look at this dancer?" He looked up. "Oh, I know!" He grabbed ahold of a nearby tree limb and climbed atop.

Isaiah felt both anger and embarrassment running the

length of his body. Though Muggy had done things like this since they were knee-high, he'd never experienced this feeling before. The undeniable instinct to physically fight his best friend.

Isaiah glanced over at Angel and Deacon Yancey, expecting them to be mortified by the idiot climbing trees and loudly disrespecting her, but they were deep in conversation. Squinting at them, Isaiah saw disgust on the deacon's face. He looked to be talking about something (or someone) he loathed, maybe even warning Angel about it. She, however, looked just as she had the day before.

Sure, she wasn't wearing a white gown; her clothing looked like she'd been dressed long before dawn—wrinkled, overlong navy skirt with a white shirt tucked underneath, and worn-out church shoes. Her hair was braided down into two chunky rows, and her face was completely free of makeup, greased down with one of the butters. She was hiding, he thought, effectively so, too. No one outside of Mount Zion Sunday school could ever imagine the music underneath. She was more than any other girls within Greenwood limits. Beyond more. And more by a lot. He couldn't believe he hadn't noticed it before. Now that he'd seen her, the real her, stripped down, he would never be able to unsee her. After yesterday, she couldn't hide from him if she tried.

"Isaiah!" yelled Muggy. "Have you heard a single word I said? You're stuck on this girl, aren't you? Wait just one damn minute," Muggy said with a shocked smile. "Is Angel Hill the dame you've been daydreaming about? What kind of magic does this dancer have to make you fall so fast?"

As Muggy jumped down from the tree with one hop, Isaiah grabbed ahold of his forearm. Muggy was a notorious hothead who never made threats that he didn't back up with action. He was born who he was, impulsive and mean, and for Isaiah to exist in his company, he had to transform himself into the same. That was the very nature of their friendship—Isaiah did as Muggy told him to do or else. Greenwood took care of its own, but even here, there was a social contract. And between Muggy and Isaiah, Muggy's family wealth gave him the upper hand. Isaiah didn't see any choice but to follow.

When Muggy wanted to blow up elderly Mr. and Mrs. Edward's mailbox in fifth grade, Isaiah lit the fuse. When Muggy locked Scott Hall in the nasty stall in sixth, Isaiah helped him barricade it shut. And when Muggy decided that Angel was unattractive, boring, and too much of a goody-goody to spend time with, Isaiah wrote her off, but not completely.

The day of the talent show, he couldn't take his eyes off of her. The way she stood. Unaffected by him or anyone else, she stood. Caring not about winning or placing or receiving applause, she stood. She stood. Just like she had in the face of the white boys who tore up her property. Angel was a Black goddess standing unseen by blind eyes. Yet Isaiah, even silently, now saw her.

Muggy punched Isaiah's shoulder. "I'm going over to tell her you like her."

But now Isaiah had a choice. Stand up to Muggy or do what he'd always done—go along to get along.

"Don't go over there, man," he told Muggy before releasing his arm. "Angel's the ugliest girl in school. Always has been. Look at her, all tall and skinny. No body. Don't get her hopes up like that."

Isaiah forced himself into a convincing laugh, and Muggy bought it hook, line, and sinker. He backed away from the fence and began walking toward the school's entrance. "I was beginning to think you lost your ever-loving mind."

"Never that," Isaiah said, catching one last look at Angel as Muggy strode ahead of him. He whispered, "I'm sorry," into the thick May air and jogged to catch up with his friend.

English literature was the only class Isaiah didn't have with Muggy. For an hour at a time, five days a week, he didn't have to deal with his best friend's cruelty, and it was refreshing. Also, his English teacher, Miss Ferris, made the class even more wonderful. On the inside, Isaiah was a poet, and Miss Ferris was the only person on earth able to tease that side of him out. He'd been written up by every teacher he'd ever had except for her.

Instead, she put a pencil in his hand and made *him* write. She'd given him a permanent pass on works like *The Scarlet*

Letter and Shakespeare. They had a no "dead white authors" agreement between the two of them. In exchange, all he had to do was fill up the leather-bound journal she'd bought for him. Since September, he'd been doing just that, and he was slowly changing on the inside. Before, he never would've gone to pre-church with his mother. And he never would have had the opportunity to see pure beauty dancing a few feet in front of him.

Isaiah was angry. Frustrated about parents and girls and the submissiveness around him, waiting unarmed to be destroyed by those on the outside. Isaiah often watched from his bedroom as Greenwood went on about its business of existing in conjunction with the untouchable white world just across the thin tracks. That, after all, was the very nature of his district—to exist in concurrence with everyone else.

Before he died, Isaiah's father had told him that Greenwood itself grew out of necessity. Oil brought the white folks, he'd told Isaiah, and whites and Native Americans brought the Black folks. But they didn't anticipate the ingenuity of *us*. We built our paradise, he'd told Isaiah, and, son, you better believe they'll want it back one day.

Isaiah was conflicted. To get along, he needed to be what was expected of him—strong, protective, no show whatsoever of weakness. But then he saw Angel dance and something cracked his resolve.

Before he saw Angel dance, waking up to face the day was a challenge. Before he saw Angel dance, going to sleep to say goodbye to the day was equally difficult. Everything in between too hard. Angel was the bolt of lightning, and poetry was the conduit, channeling all of that raw energy into tangible words. Something softened in him, and it felt good to not be so hard all the time.

"Isaiah." Miss Ferris broke his concentration. "Would you care to share one of your poems with the class?"

When he shook his head, she moved on to Annie Carlson without pressure. He'd only shared his poetry once at that same talent show, and afterward, Muggy gave him a hard time for months. He never planned to share any poems again, especially not now.

As Annie read her poem about remembering the month of November or something like that, Isaiah flipped to a fresh page in his journal and began writing.

Black Angel
Spin, spin, Black angel, spin,
Until the world no longer makes sense,
To boys or to men,
Love, spin.
Around you go,
Making me confused, lost, slow.
Around you go,
Black angel, spin.
Deep skin,
Deeper than the deepest deep,

Deeper than me,
Better, too.
Deserve you, Love, I don't,
We both know.
Don't stop spinning for me,
Black angel, but I've stopped spinning
    for you.

Isaiah finished his poem as soon as the bell rang, but he wasn't ready to leave. He felt more words in his gut, eager to rise up into his fingers and out through his pencil. He wanted another safe hour to write about Angel. Away from Muggy's prying eyes. Reluctantly, he tucked his journal into his bag and got up.

"Isaiah," Miss Ferris called out after him. "Got a minute?"

Relief came over him. A few more moments of freedom to be who he was.

"Ma'am?"

Over her green glasses, Miss Ferris looked through him as if she were reading something new and refreshing in his eyes. She took a seat behind her wooden desk and placed her chin in clasped hands.

"Something's going on with you," she said with a knowing grin. "Tell me what it is."

Instead of answering, Isaiah lifted the journal from his bag, opened the page to the newly minted poem, and slid it across her desk. She pushed her glasses farther up her nose and read. Isaiah watched her eyes slowly scan each line, and every time they did, they filled up a little more with tears. By the end, she was absolutely crying. Sobbing actually.

Miss Ferris had always been easy to cry. Not in a weak way, but in an artistic, vulnerable way. Every once in a while, Isaiah would catch her tearing up in class when they read aloud passages from the abolitionist journals or any works by Frances Ellen Watkins Harper, especially the most vivid account of slave auction or motherhood within the body of slavery. Miss Ferris felt the world with her whole heart, refusing to conform to what was expected of her as a figure of authority. Isaiah wanted to be more like Miss Ferris.

"You're in love," she said slowly and deliberately. "You should know that."

Isaiah took a moment to think before replying. He wasn't sure if he was in love or not. How could he be, after all? This was Angel. Bible-hugging Angel. Too-tall, too-skinny, too-raggedy Angel. But he couldn't stop thinking of her. When Muggy dared try to embarrass her, he thought seriously of pulling him down leg first from a tree. Since Angel stepped out of the pastor's study the day before, Isaiah couldn't stop thinking of her skin and wild hair and the way her body moved. Still, Isaiah was not prepared to make such a declaration, even to Miss Ferris.

"I don't know," he said to Miss Ferris.

"My dear boy," she replied, her chin quivering. "You're a poet, and you're in love. These two things together create the truest of art. A love like that could shift the atmosphere."

A soft knock made Miss Ferris and Isaiah both jump. Angel Hill stood in the doorway, peeking over her large glasses.

"Am I interrupting?"

Isaiah heard her words sung as a melody, the syllables coming through her like ripples in the ocean, replacing the stale air with the breathable kind. Miss Ferris looked from Isaiah to Angel and finally to his open journal. Then she knowingly closed it and handed it back to him.

"Not at all, Angel," Miss Ferris said. "I wanted to meet with both of you."

ANGEL

ny small benefit of the doubt that Isaiah Wilson pos-
sessed even an inkling of goodness escaped Angel as
soon as she saw Miss Ferris crying. How could he be so cruel
to everyone? She was Angel's favorite teacher—both brilliant and patient—she deserved awards, not tears inflicted by
spiteful, vindictive, heartless boys like him.

Muggy was a bully, plain and simple. Angel understood
bullies. At least Muggy held a discernible title, but Isaiah was
a disciple to the bully, and that she could not abide. Now, it
seemed, Isaiah was the one doing the bullying, and to sweet
Miss Ferris no less.

As he sat there with Miss Ferris, watching her with his
large, unassuming eyes, she knew what was behind them—a

hanger-on with no mind of his own taking advantage of the weak.

"Are you all right?" Angel asked her teacher while eyeing Isaiah, daring him to say a hateful word.

Angel detested confrontation, but she was put on this earth to help people and poor Miss Ferris, in that moment, needed her to be strong, to take a stand. Isaiah looked away, breaking her gaze. Coward, she thought. So big and bad when it's just Miss Ferris, but can't take on two at a time, can you?

"I'm fine," Miss Ferris replied, still wiping jumbo tears from her shiny, rose-colored cheeks. "Better than fine."

Denial, Angel thought, *that's the first sign.*

"Uh," Isaiah uttered, seemingly unable to spit out his harsh words under the weight of her gaze. "I mean, uhh."

Miss Ferris laughed, an unexpected type of snort that made her nose run. "I brought you two here to ask if you're interested in a summer job?"

"Together?" Isaiah shook his head to gather himself. "Both of us, together? Uh."

"What kind of job?" asked Angel.

"Yeah," he agreed. "That's what I was trying to—Never mind."

"I'm building a mobile library of sorts," their teacher said, smiling, but still teary. "Well, really, it's a three-wheeled bike pulling a wooden cart behind it. I'll need someone to pedal and a rider to hand out the books. There are a few challenging blocks within Greenwood. Those without formal education. I believe we can reach them through the written word, and you two love words more than any students I've ever had the pleasure of teaching. I can pay five dollars a week to each of you, equal pay of course. It is, after all, the twenties." She winked.

Five dollars a week was a generous amount. Very generous. Angel looked over at Isaiah and could tell by his wide eyes that he was thinking the same. But working together? That was a blaring problem. Angel had no desire to be in such close quarters with him, alone in thick, uncomfortable silence, without joy and goodness. Then, she remembered, Miss Ferris had mentioned that Isaiah loved words. Strange, Angel had no knowledge of this.

"I'd love to!" Isaiah said with more excitement than Angel expected. He was practically bouncing as he looked at her. "If you do, of course."

Angel wanted to tell them no. Isaiah would make fun of her once they started their shifts. It was no wonder he was so excited. He wanted a punching bag, a dumb Dora, a pushover to make him feel bigger than he actually was. Someone to direct his pent-up meanness to throughout the heat of summer. Just that day, Deacon Yancey told her to keep her distance, and he wouldn't have said it without good reason. And Isaiah and Muggy proved the deacon's point by pointing and laughing at her while she sat on his porch. What, did Isaiah think she hadn't seen them?

But then, five whole dollars a week. She could save every bit of that for her family. And, she'd be handing out books.

Helping people fall in love with them in the same way she had so many years ago. That sounded like pure joy. She felt a tug happening on the inside, but neither side was winning.

"I'd like to think about it," Angel said. "Thank you, Miss Ferris, for the opportunity. Can I let you know tomorrow?"

Angel decided it would be a good idea to take the long way home. She needed time to think about what she was going to do. The seesaw of emotion at the thought of dealing with Isaiah confused her. She thought she had everyone in Greenwood pretty well figured out. She had observed and categorized those she should and should not share her audience with. Isaiah was undoubtedly trouble.

Then again, was that the right thing to do? Funnel folks into columns marked good and bad without taking nuance into consideration? Did everyone do that, or was it just her? This was one of the moments she longed for a friend or a sister— someone to run her thoughts by. But there was only her— independent to her own detriment. And she couldn't bother her father with every confusing philosophical thought as she had in the past. He was barely hanging on as it was. So she did the one thing within her power; she prayed for answers. She didn't ask for anything too profound or specific, just signs and answers.

As she turned the corner leading to her house, she heard baby Michael yelling and quickened her step to get to him.

"Amen," she said to herself, and then called out, "Mrs. Nichelle?"

Angel pushed in the screen to find her neighbor on the couch holding Michael with one exhausted arm. "Go to bed," Angel told her. "I've got the baby until you wake up."

Mrs. Nichelle looked too tired to smile. She lifted her tiny body like it was weighted down by a thousand pounds and went into her bedroom.

"I'll take him next door."

Angel went into her own home through the back as not to disturb her father, who was typically dozing on the couch by that time of day. Her mother greeted her with a kiss on the cheek as soon as she entered.

"Sweet of you to keep him," her mother said. "Little demon child won't stop his screaming."

Angel quickly covered the baby's ears. "Mama!"

"What?" she replied, grinning. "It's the truth."

Her mother cleared a place on the dining room table and lined up a variety of hair greases. "Better get him quiet quick," she told Angel. "I've got to do three whole heads of braids by midnight, and I'll need you to help."

"Yes, ma'am," Angel replied. "The Barney sisters?"

"That's right," said her mother with a strong sigh. "I hope you're ready for a dramatic evening filled with unnecessary hooping and hollering."

"But we just did their hair Saturday."

"Their mama said they got to rolling in mud," her mother said. "They need a wash and deep condition."

"Angel!" her dad called out. "Get in here."

Her mother paused to look at her daughter with pity. Angel could tell her mother didn't want so much responsibility on her shoulders. Angel nodded as if encouraging her mother to carry on.

"How about a dollar fifteen this time?" her mother asked, and when Angel smiled, she went back to laying out long ribbons and wide-toothed combs. "Best go in there to see what he wants," she said with a wink.

ISAIAH

Muggy demanded to walk Isaiah home that afternoon. He wanted to tell Isaiah about a girl he'd kissed after school behind the wooden bleachers, and how she'd wanted to do much more but Muggy was playing with her. This was a broken record that Isaiah listened to on frequent repeat. There was always a new girl to kiss, and a new game to win, and a new story to tell, and a new heart to shatter. Isaiah stopped listening altogether as they walked past Angel's house. He slyly tried to catch a glimpse of her through one of the windows without Muggy noticing. He certainly couldn't know that Isaiah hadn't stopped thinking of her and the way she danced. He would laugh, or worse, tell her, or worse, tell all of Greenwood.

Isaiah had seen the way Angel looked at him when Miss

Ferris proposed they work together after school. Utter disgust. But he expected no less after all the hell Muggy made him put her through since childhood. Muggy was the root of the problem, absolutely. He glared at him as Muggy walked ahead—one hand emoting his words and the other holding on tight to his unlit cigar. Isaiah was sick and tired of Muggy Little Jr., but Muggy was Greenwood royalty. Without him, what would Isaiah be? Nothing. Nobody. All alone and outcast in their town.

"What kind of square rides around on a bike handing out books?" Muggy asked, breaking the silence. "It's stupid if you ask me."

Isaiah stayed quiet, because it wasn't stupid. It wasn't stupid at all. Actually, it was brilliant. Square or not square, books changed lives. Books had absolutely changed his. He hid his reading in the same way he hid his poetry, and now, his angel. Hiding his passions from Muggy was becoming a hallmark of their so-called friendship.

"You said no to Miss Ferris, right?" Muggy continued. "It's stupid," he repeated. "And why on earth wouldn't she ask me to join in? I'm as smart as you are."

Isaiah shrugged without confirming or denying. But of course he'd said yes. What was he supposed to do? Walk around Greenwood with Muggy every day for the rest of his life, chasing girls with nothing valuable to talk about? Muggy was the stupid one, skipping high school, while Isaiah, again secretly, was ranked in the top-tenth percentile overall. The only thing keeping Muggy from being kicked out of Booker T. Washington was his wealthy father, a butcher whose shop customers, both Black and white, traveled far and wide for the very best cuts of meat.

Thankfully, they approached Isaiah's house before Muggy had a chance to ask again. Isaiah quickly walked to his porch and waved. "See you tomorrow morning."

He closed the door behind him and let out an exasperated huff.

"I don't know why you associate with him," Isaiah's mother said as soon as the door shut. "You're better than that."

Isaiah didn't know, either.

"Hungry?"

He dropped his satchel in the foyer and followed his mother into their spotless kitchen. The warm smell of caramelized onions filled his nose and made his eyes itch; it was his father's favorite, beef and onions.

Isaiah wanted to talk to his dad about Angel. His father used to be the town's authority on such things, listening to everyone's problems and solving them as if it were the easiest thing in the world. Isaiah loved him. His mother loved him. But everyone who met him, too, even in passing, fell for his quick wit and wisdom. The day he boarded the train for the big war, it seemed as if the entire district waved him on his way. Isaiah could remember the whites of hands as far as he could see, fluttering in their direction. The whole of Greenwood respected his father, and the whole of Greenwood mourned when he didn't come home.

But he'd been gone a while now. So long, in fact, that Isaiah was starting to kick himself for forgetting the little things about him—his voice, his eyes, his infectious laugh. Most of all, he was beginning to forget his father's aphorisms. His father could pull the appropriate saying without skipping a single beat, showering wisdom onto anyone who sought him out for it. Some inexplicably branded themselves into Isaiah's mind—when cobwebs are plenty kisses are scarce, gluttony kills more than the sword, and a friend to all is a friend to none. But Isaiah could think of none to help him with his Angel dilemma.

"Mom," Isaiah said, watching her spoon generous helpings of beef and onions into two porcelain bowls. "Can I ask you something?"

"Anything, baby." She sat across from him and clasped her waiting hands.

"What do you know about Angel Hill?"

He watched his mother's hands come apart and shoot to the ceiling in celebration. "Angel Hill?" she nearly shouted. "Down the way? My God, he's asking about Angel Hill."

Isaiah lowered his head. "That's why I didn't want to talk to you about this. I knew you'd make a fuss."

"I'm sorry," she said, but the energy in the kitchen had shifted. She was all bouncing knees and twitchy cheeks, wanting so badly to smile ear to ear. "Just . . . Angel Hill is . . ."

"An angel?"

"Well . . . ," she started. "Yes, as close to one as humanly possible, I'd say."

She is, he thought, visualizing her spinning in white.

"I'll never understand how she goes overlooked in this town," his mother added, shaking her head.

Again, he thought the same. Yet he'd been so very cruel.

"Not just overlooked, Mama. We were awful to her," Isaiah started before he'd realized. "*I* was awful to her."

Isaiah looked up to see the question in his mother's eyes— why? He decided to answer it before she had an opportunity to ask.

"Because . . . ," he said, head hung low. "She seemed an easy target, I suppose. No fight in her."

His mother laughed but not in a humorous way. "Oh, dear boy. That's where you're more wrong than you know."

His mother didn't have to speak her disdain for him in that moment; a son can read that in shrug of shoulders and tone of voice. Isaiah hung his head so low now that his forehead nearly brushed his dinner.

"Sorry, Mama."

"Ah," she said, still angry but slightly softened. "No need to say sorry. You, dear boy, will live. And as you do, you will have to look back to see that the real fighters only open their mouths when it is absolutely necessary. The Muggy Little

Juniors speak through their own insecurities and say the wrong damn thing in the process."

It was the first time he'd ever heard his mother say a curse word of any kind. And it made Isaiah feel like the villain of his own story. He spooned his beef and onions without eating it, knowing full well it was moist and delicious, but he couldn't take a bite. He disgusted himself.

"I've been," he started. "I've been . . ."

Somewhere between his mind and the world, the words got stuck. He didn't want to disappoint his kind, delicate mother. She, too, was too good for him. All sweet, no bitter. He'd been cruel to her. Not in the same way he'd been to Angel, but in other ways.

He'd left his mother to cry alone. He'd heard her—night after night—through their thin walls. Once, he'd quietly walked into the kitchen to find her sobbing over the sink. He easily could have placed his palm on her back. Even, dear Lord, cried right along with her. But, no. He'd walked by without a single word or touch, leaving her all alone.

Alone she was, clinging firmly to the thought that she'd see her beloved husband again one day on the other side of heaven. But lonely still. Figuring creative ways to feed, clothe, and house her ungrateful upchuck of a son.

"You've been what?"

He wanted to tell her how horrible he'd been over the years. To please Muggy, he justified. To fit in, he could argue. But not really. He had no one to blame but himself for being unworthy of Angel and his mother, too. He couldn't find the way to say such things aloud, though.

"I'd like to come with you to Sunday school again this week if you don't mind," he said as he shoved a heaping spoonful into his mouth. Dinner was even better than he'd expected it to be.

His mother beamed in response.

After dinner, he lay across his bed with his journal in his hands, his mind blank of anything to write. He was frozen there with an empty brain. He felt under his pillow for *The Souls of Black Folk* and found it, well-read and worn.

Like a Bible, the book usually opened directly to where he needed it to go. When the uniformed men had shown up on his doorstep to tell them of his father's death, the book opened to the section entitled "Of the Passing of the First-Born." He decided to reread that passage:

> He died at eventide, when the sun lay like a
> brooding sorrow above the western hills, veiling
> its face; when the winds spoke not, and the trees,
> the great green trees he loved, stood motionless. I
> saw his breath beat quicker and quicker, pause,
> and then his little soul leapt like a star that
> travels in the night and left a world of darkness
> in its train. The day changed not; the same
> tall trees peeped in at the windows, the same

green grass glinted in the setting sun. Only in
the chamber of death writhed the world's most
piteous thing—a childless mother.

That passage spoke deeper to Isaiah's heart than any well-wisher's condolence. Such things could only be written by someone who knew the heavy weight of true loss. Like Du Bois articulated miraculously, the shocking death of a loved one isn't a wailing thing. The real shudder comes from the world moving on as if nothing's happened. Shops flip their Closed signs to Open, patrons gather at the theaters and soda shops, and people dare smile at things that make them happy, while those left in the ruins find joy in nothing.

A tiny rock hit the sill of his bedroom window. For a moment, he thought it might be Angel. Then he caught himself in the dream and realized it must instead be Dorothy Mae.

She'd been voted Most Beautiful last year, even though she wasn't technically allowed to be named that her sophomore year. She was an unlikely pencil-in candidate who actually won. And it was much deserved, too; Dorothy Mae was shockingly beautiful. She and Isaiah had been necking for months. Mostly touching, rarely talking. Whenever they stopped kissing, she had nothing much to say, and Isaiah would rather kiss than gossip. Besides, he was under enough pressure from Muggy to speak ill of others, he certainly didn't want to do it with her, too. So they kissed until their lips went purple and tingly. Still, he'd never written a single poem about Dorothy Mae.

"Hey," he heard her singsongy voice through his closed window.

"Damn," he said aloud, knowing what that meant. She was on her way up the leggy tree outside of his bedroom. He needed to write. Even a little, quickly. He cracked the window and began writing as she slowly and carefully climbed in her frilly dress.

> *Hey there, Miss miss:*
> *Please stay where you are,*
> *Miss miss, you don't know me at all.*
> *Don't throw rocks, don't kiss.*
> *No offense, Miss miss,*
> *But there's better than this,*
> *Much better, there's bliss.*
> *Miss miss, I like,*
> *Black Angel, I love, Miss miss, I need you to*
>   *know.*
> *Please go, Miss miss.*
> *You'll be somebody's Mrs.*
> *Not mine, Miss miss.*
> *Not even close.*

There. He'd written his first poem about Dorothy Mae, and while it wasn't anything special, it revealed how he truly felt about her on the hidden inside. As poetry does.

Isaiah heard a small rasping sound on his bedroom window. It was Dorothy Mae's bright pink manicured fingernail scraping a heart against the glass. He shut his journal and walked over to raise his window so she could clamber inside.

"Come in," he said, trying to sound light and airy while feeling heavy with grief and craving for someone the polar opposite to Dorothy Mae.

He slid the window down after her and stared at her for a brief moment, hoping she'd say something worth hearing.

As she leaned in to kiss him, he dodged. "Have a seat," he said, bouncing around the bed like a kangaroo. "I have to run to the toilet."

He didn't have to go to the toilet at all. He just needed time to think and analyze his own reflection in the mirror. "Come on, man," he told himself. "The town Sheba's in your bed."

But his body reacted in ways it never had before. Tiny beads of sweat seeped from his neat hairline and dried before they reached his brow. His bottom lip trembled like he wanted to vomit. And his right hand shook with the instinct to write, or maybe to read; either way, he wanted to disappear somehow into words. To forget the predicament he found himself in.

Looking in the mirror, he saw weakness all over him. Too weak to tell a beautiful young woman in the next room that he was no longer interested in her and that maybe he never had been. Bank's closed! He should've been brave enough to say aloud but wasn't. Simultaneously, he was too weak to release such feelings and fade away into the desires of every man his age. *Just kiss the broad. What are you, lame?* Muggy would've surely asked him. And yes would certainly be the answer. He was lame.

He exhaled loudly at the mirror. "Come on, Isaiah," he said. "Come! On!"

But there was no use. He simply did not want Dorothy Mae any longer. He wanted Angel, and if he couldn't have her, he wanted to devour words on a page. He closed his eyes and attempted to focus his confused mind.

The hardest of truths was that the conflict inside him was placed on him by humanity, and the deepest weakness was he wanted to succumb to it. To give in to the perception of what society thought he should be—more like Muggy Little Jr.— interested only in the pleasures of now and uncaring for the steadiness of his people's future. He wasn't like Du Bois at all. He wasn't even like Booker T. Washington. No revolutionary cared so much how they were seen within the flawed world. They only cared for repairing it. They would lay down their lives to make an attempt at valuable change, not tease tears in a tiny toilet over kissing a girl.

A cry burned at the corner of Isaiah's eye, and he blinked it away before it could fully materialize.

"No!" he said to his reflection. "You will not."

He closed his eyes and searched his mind for an appropriate segment from *Souls* to distract him. When he thought of one, he reopened his eyes and unblinkingly recited it to himself:

"'*He began to have a dim feeling that, to attain his place in the world, he must be himself, and not another . . . He began to have a dim feeling that, to attain his place in the world, he must be himself, and not another . . . He began to have a dim feeling that, to attain his place in the world, he must be himself, and not another.'"*

He lost count of how many times he'd said it. He would've continued, but he heard a small, concerned knock on the door.

"You okay in there, baby?" his mother said softly.

He blinked at her sweet voice. "I'm okay!" he lied. "Be out soon."

With one last look, he threw a cold splash of water on his face and considered the words he'd repeated over and over. Profound, strong, true, and wholly empty when spoken aloud by Isaiah himself. They needed a revolutionary to speak them, someone worthy, not him. Words alone held no sway. They didn't carry whips and chains, or yell halt to adversaries without someone worthy to speak them.

So with one last breath, he forced himself to go back into his room to kiss the girl he didn't want to kiss.

ANGEL

"Hey, my angel," said Angel's father through broken breaths. "And there's my sweet boy."

Her father held his arms open for baby Michael, and just like before, he fell into them. The same calm knowing came over Michael, and it made Angel want to cry. She knew that her father was right, but didn't want to accept it. The child knew something about her father that she couldn't know. Her instinct was to snatch the baby away. It was too obvious when they were together—new life and impending death, sitting at the opposite ends of their journeys, greeting one another with a mutually earned respect that she couldn't bear to acknowledge.

Angel wanted her father alive. She wanted both of her parents, walking hand in hand like they used to. Supporting one another. Holding each other up in life and health and strength, never in sickness. The knock on the door made her shoulders jump and snapped her out of whatever she was in. It was her mother's four o'clock hair appointment—the tender-headed Barney twins plus one. Angel was beginning to think their mother was sending them just to get a break from their chaos. Odd of the sisters to knock on the front door. They usually burst directly into the back as if they owned the place.

"I'll get it," said Angel, looking back at her father. "Don't worry, I'll walk them around back. You okay with Michael?"

"Thanks," he said, relieved to not have to shift himself out of their chaotic way. "Yes, I've got Little Man."

Angel cracked the front door, and to her surprise, Muggy Little Jr. was standing there holding a brown leather-bound journal in his hands, grinning mischievously.

"I've got something to show you," he said with a sly wink.

ISAIAH

Isaiah's lips had gone all tingly, but Dorothy Mae was still lapping them with full lungs. She smelled nice—like fake flowers. Had to be a lotion of some kind, because as her hands, then wrists, then forearm, then armpit brushed close to his nose, the smell stayed the same. Bored of kissing, he tried to ease her away gently. She was a girl, after all. One with an assertive way about her—like a fake flower.

"Don't stop," she whispered into his neck before kissing it.

She sounded like a picture-show girlfriend, not a real one. Like she'd rehearsed "don't stop" to her own reflection to make it sound authentic. As he knew her, that summed her up. Isaiah wondered what she was like when she was alone—when she first stepped out of the bath. Smelling only of basic soap and hard Greenwood water, not fake anything.

He wondered, did she wipe the condensation away from the mirror to stare herself down or did she walk past it unwilling to truly see herself as she was, regular. Beautiful, but regular, just like him. Still, Isaiah wanted to believe there was depth underneath all the vapid.

He pushed her away so hard she couldn't deny he wanted to stop. "Let's talk awhile."

"Talk?" she replied. "Whatever do you mean?"

"I mean"—Isaiah scooted back, putting enough distance between them that she couldn't lunge onto his sore lips— "what's your favorite color?"

"Don't be a flat tire, Isaiah," she said, nervously picking at her pink polish. "Who cares what my favorite color is?"

"I wouldn't have asked if I didn't care, but okay, I'll start," he began. "Mine is obviously blue." He pointed to the colored paper on his bedroom walls and wondered if she'd ever even noticed.

She looked around and half smiled. "Huh."

Silence fell hard on his bedroom, slowly stacking a thousand invisible bricks between them in his small bed.

"Want to hear a quick passage from my favorite book?" he asked, pulling *Souls* from underneath his pillow. "I don't know if you follow Du Bois." He paused. "Do you?"

"I don't follow politics."

Isaiah laughed. "Du Bois is not just politics. He's starting a revolution for our people. Real change, not that flimsy stuff Booker T. used to preach. This is taking our power back from the white man. Standing firmly on our feet and telling the world that we've earned the right to exist. Listen to this!"

Dorothy Mae held her hand in the air, halting Isaiah.

"I like Booker T. Washington, though," Dorothy Mae began, her brow creased. "I don't like when people disparage him for his methods. He did the very best he could under the circumstances of his birth and region."

Isaiah grinned. "I thought you didn't follow politics," he said, noticing a fresh zeal in her eyes, finally a reveal of an opinion about something important. "You should show more of this."

"I . . . ," she started, and got stuck in the beginning of the sentence. "I meant that I follow politics just fine, I just . . . How should I say? It's not expected of me to speak my opinions aloud. I'm meant to marry well, not express my like or disdain for the revolutionaries among us."

And that's when Isaiah pinpointed the elusive thing he liked about Dorothy Mae—born to a wealthy-bank-owner father and a former-beauty-queen mother, she was just as trapped in expectation as he was. Hers was the expectation of marrying well within Greenwood society. Utilizing her radiance to charm herself into cushy sitting rooms with cut glass and tiny sandwiches.

"Okay." He joined her back on his bed. "Indulge me for one more question."

"Just one if you please."

"What do you dream of becoming?" he asked before again

shooting to his feet to pace the room. "Not 'What do you want to be when you grow up?' I hate when teachers ask such questions. No! I mean, when you lie down on your pillow, alone and free, what do you dream of becoming?"

She looked at him skeptically, like she was afraid to be honest with him. Almost ashamed. "Father says I should—"

"No," Isaiah interrupted. "Not what father says. What you say! What you think!"

With eyes like saucers, she opened her mouth and closed it four times before she found the courage to speak. "No one's ever thought to ask what I want to be. Maybe never in my life. I'm not sure how to . . ."

"The truth as it exists in your heart, Dorothy Mae." Isaiah beamed, finally feeling some semblance of connection to her.

"You can't tell anyone."

Isaiah held his palm to the sky. "You have my word."

She leaned back on his pillow and stared at the ceiling, allowing herself, for the first time, to slouch. "I want to fly."

Isaiah didn't laugh, not even a little. He did, however, sit back on his bed and lean in close to her. "That's the Dorothy Mae I want to hear about. Tell me everything."

Then she stood to her feet, shedding her posture completely. "I don't care how I get up there, Isaiah, I just want to be as close to the clouds as possible. Is that dumb?"

"I think this is the first not-dumb thing I've ever heard you say."

"Hey!" she shouted playfully.

"It's the truth," he said, equally spirited. "All that talk about the weather and dinner parties. That's dumb. But this? This is quite the opposite. This is the talk of a woman whose more than the weather or who sits where at the dining table. More than fringe and feathers. This, dear, is the talk of a dreamer."

She sat back down on the bed, this time right next to him. More like a friend than a lover. "You're a strange one. I hope you know that, Isaiah Wilson."

"You know what, Dorothy Mae?" he asked. "I have a sneaking feeling that you might be, too. Way down deep."

"It's time for me to ask you a question now."

"Anything at all."

"Why don't *you* show anyone who you actually are?" she asked. "You're just as phony as you're implying I am."

"First of all," he started. "I did not call you phony."

"You didn't have to," she interrupted.

"Fair enough," he gave in. "I'll own that I'm usually putting on. I'm only real when I write. Can I read you one of my poems?"

He felt behind him, where he knew he'd left it, but it wasn't there. Then he crouched down to look under his bed for his leather journal.

"Stand up a minute," he told her, before tearing through his pillows and wildly unmaking his bed. "It has to be here."

"What?"

"My journal," he said, appearing to get frantic. "The one I always carry with me. Have you seen it?"

Dorothy Mae looked curious at the question. "I have to go," she said instead of answering. "I have to go," she repeated. And she was out the window before he could ask why.

ANGEL

"Muggy?" Angel stepped onto the porch to join him. "What are you doing here?"

Muggy Little Jr. turned his back to her and walked to the swinging bench at the far end of her large porch. "Sit," he said before patting the empty space beside him.

"I have chores," she started. "My papa . . . No, my mama needs me to help with a hair appointment . . . and baby Michael."

"I'll make it worth your while," he said with a rascally grin. "Worth the sacrifice of missing some little chores."

She stood over him, knowing he had no clue what he was talking about. Some little chores, she thought, included helping her mother clean her father's excrement, bathe and shift him to avoid festering sores, and help him fight for a will to live. Muggy Little Jr. was the worst hue of green—still naive and entitled but also with an air of grandiosity. He knew nothing beyond himself and cared not to find out. She'd hate to see where life actually took him in the end. Nowhere positive, she surmised.

"Okay," he continued, striking a match to light his dangling cigar. "Not going to sit? Suit yourself."

"Please don't light that," she told him. "Not here. It's not good for my papa."

Ignoring her, he opened the journal and began quietly paging through it.

"My apologies, Muggy," she said, backing toward her front door. "I don't have time for—"

"'*Black Angel,*'" he started reading. *"By Isaiah Wilson. Spin, spin, Black angel, spin . . .'"*

As he read the poem aloud, right there on the sweltering Greenwood afternoon, Angel felt herself leaning against the railings of her porch. Her eyes went from angry and frustrated to kind and soft. She noticed the verbena again, even brighter than they had been that morning. Showing off for the sun and God and herself.

She felt her father, dying of an unknown illness in the next room. Fighting so valiantly just to sit up straight in her presence. Connecting more with beautiful new babies than with anyone else now. She felt her mother, robustly braiding away the pain in their small kitchen. Twisting the smallest of braids for something to focus on outside of the failing health of the love of her life, the father of her best friend.

She felt her hands shaking like they did before she was about to cry. She tasted heavy tears that couldn't break through until she'd heard the perfect poem about her spinning in the pulpit. Then she saw the strange sight of Dorothy Mae, dressed in fuzzy pink, running up her walkway.

"Give it to me," Dorothy told Muggy furiously. "This is not your business to tell."

"Whoa, now," he said, holding the journal high in the air and out of her reach. "You're the one who handed it to me through Isaiah's window just, what, a half hour ago? What the hell are you even talking about? I think this is the first time I've ever heard you speak." He went to grab her around the waist for a kiss, but she wouldn't allow it.

"Muggy," she said to him. "This is wrong."

He laughed in response. "Wrong, right, who the hell cares? It's fun. Besides, I've already read her one of my favorites. Take it." He handed the journal to Dorothy Mae and rested his attention on Angel. "Now you know, Black Angel. Do with it what you will." He walked to the sidewalk and tipped his hat, leaving Angel and Dorothy Mae on the porch.

"Angel," her father called out from the living room. "Who's out there? Are you okay? I can come help if you need me."

In a panic, Angel nearly tripped over her own feet heading for the door. "No, Papa, please don't try to get up. Please."

As she opened the door, she looked back at Dorothy Mae holding the journal. Dorothy had caught full sight of Angel's once-strong father, withering on the couch. Angel shut the door, but it was too late; she'd already seen him.

"I'm . . . ," Dorothy Mae began speaking. "I'm so sorry."

Then she ran away.

ISAIAH

"**M**om!" Isaiah called out, flipping and re-flipping over the same bedspread, and turning his pillowcases inside out for the thirteenth time. "Have you seen my journal?" Isaiah was now in a full terror.

"No, baby," she said. "You had it when you came in."

He knew he'd had it. That's what made it so odd. Isaiah always knew where his journal was. It was a treasure trove of anger and frustration and love. He'd written multiple poems about how much he deeply despised Muggy and the Greenwood hierarchy. And then there was the new, raw love in there. He'd never live that down. Moreover, his personal statements for Howard and Morehouse were in there, and not yet transcribed onto full-length parchment. Those letters were perfect and whole, impossible to duplicate.

"I can't find it!" he shouted into the ether. Not necessarily to his mother.

"You need me to help you look?"

"No," he said to her, flailing his hands.

"Retrace your steps."

She was right. He sat on the now-mussed bed, closed his eyes, and visualized himself through the afternoon.

He saw himself walking in, longing to talk to his father and settling for his mother. He recalled her excitement over Angel Hill and smiled. He couldn't blame her. If he had a son one day who'd expressed interest in a girl like that, he'd be excited, too. She was a universe of a girl, overlooked like a daily sunset. His finger itched to write, reminding him to concentrate on his lost journal.

After talking to his mom, he went into his room. With closed eyes, he saw himself writing on his bed with his journal resting on his bent knees. He couldn't remember how much time had passed before Dorothy Mae had traced that heart on his window, but he'd absolutely had his journal in his room. They fooled around awhile, like always, and that's when the journal left his memories. He felt a stick to his upper thigh—the tip of the ink pen he'd held when writing in it.

"Dammit, Dorothy," he said.

ISAIAH

The sun rose the following morning, but Isaiah hadn't slept a single wink. He'd barely blinked since realizing Dorothy Mae had stolen the only thing that shouldn't be stolen. His mind was woolly with worry and questions. What could she possibly want with it? Why would she steal something so personal? Who had she shown it to?

He'd spent the night answering his own questions with the worst, and most plausible, conclusion—Muggy was behind this. Then Isaiah had to spend more hours talking himself out of it and do a roundabout right back to the same outcome—Muggy, of course. It was, after all, his style. They'd done horrible things like this together thousands of times. No one in Greenwood was safe from their mischief, but Isaiah thought his friendship was his shield. Armor from the embarrassment and pain inflicted by his best friend.

In the very journal he'd likely stolen, Isaiah wrote a poem about Muggy entitled "The Shield." It was a short burst of a poem, and if Muggy ever got his hands on it, there would be no place to hide from the wrath. Isaiah would be a lightning rod, drawing all fire from every other poor victim in Greenwood. Muggy would be relentless. Isaiah couldn't remember the poem verbatim, but he knew the circumstances in which he'd written it.

Muggy had taken a sanitary pad from a small freshman girl named Mary's open pocketbook, dipped it in ketchup, and slyly stuck it to the outside of her skirt. When she rose, he loudly, no, obnoxiously pointed and screamed, "Bloody Mary, Bloody Mary!"

It was her nickname from that moment on, and Isaiah, weakly, sadly, ashamedly, laughed along. Afterward, Isaiah peeled off to the bathroom, disappearing into a stall for privacy. That's when he took out the felt-tipped ink pen that was poking him in the thigh all night long and wrote "The Shield."

Could he have left his journal at school in his locker? That whole remembering-writing-in-it thing could've easily been yesterday or the day before. His mother was surely mistaken—no way she saw him holding it that afternoon. The days were bleeding into one another anyway. What was it? May? He was certainly mistaken.

The sun peeked over the trees in the distance, and he told himself he was worried for no reason at all. He pulled on a pair of cuffed pants and a crisp white T-shirt to wait at the curb for his best friend. The sun brightened more and more as the moments passed.

Isaiah glanced at his watch—7:36 A.M. He'd been waiting for fifteen minutes longer than usual, but surely Muggy had just overslept again, silly boy. That's all. Isaiah chuckled to himself faintly.

7:47 A.M.

7:56 A.M.

8:00 A.M.

Already late, he began walking alone.

Back and forth went his mind between overreaction and trouble. Between worst cases and best. Belonging and cast out. The what-ifs were the worst of it, he knew. The lead-up was always more dreadful than the actual event. Wasn't it?

It reminded him of the one time he entered the school-wide talent show. It wasn't worth it after all—that lack of sleep, upheaval of guts, twisting of mind. All for some measly applause and a trophy. He'd won actually. Against jugglers and sopranos and toe dancers. He'd won the whole thing with a poem about history. A poem that he'd written on a wrinkled, stained napkin moments before walking onstage. A poem that had since attached itself to his memory and never released.

To pass the time and forget his current predicament, he began to recite it to himself. Walking the smooth walkways, past Mrs. Tate's prizewinning juniper, unintentionally flailing his arms as he spoke.

"*The past is the past,*" he started in a low, growly voice he'd practiced for years. "But it's not the past just because time has passed. The past is right here in our faces. Breathing sour breath of captors on us. Enslaving the brave. Braving the shame. Shaming us away from our real African names . . ."

"I remember when you did that," someone said from behind him. "You beat me that year."

Isaiah was genuinely shocked by Angel's voice interrupting his thoughts. His mind was now empty. Void of words or thoughts. There was only Angel in the flesh. Keeping pace with his quick, tardy walk to school. He looked down at her slightly dirty white shoes. Though they were dingy and cheap, her stride in them held beauty. The worn indenture at the tip of her shoes pointed like she was floating, not walking.

He could hear himself breathing through their silence. He sounded like a raging bull, in and out and out and in. She must've been disgusted by it. Any girl would be. He held his breath for a few seconds, then choked dusty Oklahoma air into his lungs.

She laughed.

Cut by her laughter, he felt the instinct to speak in a lounge-lizard drawl he'd used on other girls. His body began to lean into a performance walk, every stride long with a catch at the end. Girls liked that, he thought. He curled his upper lip as if it were holding on to a thick cigar.

She laughed again.

Huh, he thought.

He cut his act and began walking normal again. For the first time in a while, he had no idea how to walk or talk or think. He had to lift a foot, one at a time, as if she'd made him forget the simple things about life. Every few steps, he glimpsed over at her pointed toes.

"I'm taking the job," she said.

He tripped on his feet a little as she spoke, but recovered. But his nerves kept his lips from parting to respond.

"I think it's a good opportunity," she added, clearly waiting for him to say something (anything) in response, but he couldn't. He'd just say something wrong or awkward or dumb.

"I never knew books were really your thing," she continued through the natural pause she'd given him to say something. "I suppose I should've. Your poetry is beautiful."

"How do you know my poetry?" His words came out a bit too forcefully, like caged birds breaking free one at a time.

Taken aback, she didn't reply this time.

They turned the corner toward school. He had less than a block to say something that meant something. To charm the angel he'd pushed around since they were small. To tell her how much he loved the way she danced or walked or spoke about things that mattered. Approaching the gate, he grabbed at her hand but missed. She'd walked ahead a bit and didn't notice the attempt. When he tried again, the back of his hand brushed her backside. And that she felt. Heat rose in his ears, and his stomach became instantly upset. He was such an idiot.

"I didn't . . . ," he started. "I was trying to . . . never mind that. I swear I didn't mean to." He kicked at a stray rock sitting atop the dusty earth at his feet. "You like politics?"

He really was such an idiot. A one-trick pony. A wurp. A wet blanket. Of course she didn't care about politics. She was a good Christian girl whose single dance could shift the mood of Greenwood's largest church. Such! An! Idiot!

"I do like politics, actually," she replied, kicking the rock back at his foot, challenging him to an impromptu game of rock soccer. "In the world we live in, it would be irresponsible not to."

His muddled mind didn't register her response. "Wait, what?" he asked before too-forcefully kicking the rock into her shin.

"Ouch!" She bent forward to rub at the reddening welt.

"My God," he said. "I'm so sorry . . . I didn't—" He truly, no joke, was such an idiot.

"It's okay. No break in the skin or anything," she said before rolling her skirt back down. "I like Booker T. Washington's philosophies. Smart as a whip, that one."

Isaiah's exuberance and cautiousness left his body. "No, no, no, no, no, no, no, no," he said, shaking his head back and forth. "He most definitely is not."

He knew he shouldn't challenge her so quickly, but he couldn't help it. Passion overtook him.

"Du Bois is the smart one," he told her in a lecturing tone. "Washington is weak. Have you studied Du Bois's theory of triple paradox?" Isaiah knew he should stop talking, but he couldn't seem to figure out how. "In direct response to Washington's approach, Du Bois asked which is more effective toward racial progress: submissiveness, educational advancement, or suffrage. The question is intellectually sound and perfect, very much unlike Washington's simplistic view on slow, generational progress."

A pause hung in the air between them, and Isaiah looked at his feet.

"I . . . ," Angel began. "Well, I thoughtfully and respectfully disagree with your and Du Bois's assessment."

"Which part exactly?" Isaiah itched to argue.

"That discussion is for another time," she said with a tilt of the head. "But in your short speech, I can already see that you may well believe every word from Du Bois's lips was placed there by God himself, and to that, I caution you. He is just a man. Which means he will disappoint you."

Shocked by her measured response, he felt his shoulders deflate, so he hitched them back up, forcing his spine straight and chin higher than they naturally sat. Familiar performance overtook his body, changing his posture into something closer to Muggy's than his own.

Angel quickly closed the space between them like she was about to kiss him square on the lips. He stood his ground, ready. But she didn't kiss him. She grabbed both of his hands and locked eyes with him. He saw the universe in her eyes, the sparkling universe. He itched to write that down—*sparkling universe in her eyes.* He could write pages about only her eyes, verb-filled run-on sentences about every eyelash.

"You don't have to pretend with me, Isaiah," she said, pulling his ace card with such honesty and rawness that he couldn't deny it. "Be you. That's enough for me."

She squeezed his hands once and walked through the school gates, leaving him standing there, alone and dazed.

Her breath smelled clean, like honeysuckle or maybe huckleberry. The smell lingered on the wind for a while, and Isaiah was sad when an especially hasty gust took it away. He knew right then that he was madly, truly, singularly in love with Angel Hill.

"You're a fool to like her," Muggy said as he jumped down from the nearby tree limb. The same kind of perch he'd been spying on her in the day before. "And an even bigger fool to leave this on your bed with a floozy nearby."

Muggy tossed the leather-bound journal high. Isaiah watched it flip through the air as if it were moving in slow motion. He caught it and saw a page was aggressively folded down. He opened the journal to that particular place—it was the poem he'd written about Muggy.

> ### The Shield
> *I hate him he's my shield,*
> *His filthy, rotting guts,*
> *He's cruel but he's my shield,*

He's built me from the bottom up.
I'll use him,
I swear,
And leave him when I'm good enough,
To stand alone,
Without him, Dear God, that day can't
    come soon enough.
I'll be, one day.
Shieldless,
Muggyless,
One day.
A Proud.
Poet.

"That one's my favorite," Muggy said before leaning against the tree's thick trunk. "Even though the end doesn't rhyme, which, what rhymes with 'Muggyless'?" Isaiah caught quick eyes with Dorothy Mae, who was waiting in the nearby bushes with her head bent with shame, her face in her hands.

ANGEL

"I'll do it!" Angel burst into Miss Ferris's classroom. "When do we get started?"

"Now," Miss Ferris replied with her hands raised, "this is a quick turn of events. What's changed?"

Angel didn't want to admit it. Honestly, she wasn't sure what she'd be admitting to in the first place. Isaiah had written the most beautiful poem about her, that was true, but that wasn't the whole reason she'd changed her mind. There was also her father. She wanted to ease the stress of their small home. Her mother's wrists were in constant pain from too much hair braiding, and he'd voluntarily skipped a few medications to make the monthlies.

On top of all of this, though, was a selfish longing to get away from it all, and she hated herself for thinking it. She was put on this earth to help people—from her colicky infant neighbor to her ailing father. It was her purpose. When she was very small, Angel dreamed only of taking care of others. For the first time, she wanted a few hours per day to do only the thing she wanted to do.

"I could use the money." She told the half-truth to a skeptical-looking Miss Ferris. "I could use the money," she echoed herself before kicking an invisible ball at her feet.

"O-kay," Miss Ferris replied in huffing disbelief. She then looked at her watch. "We have a few minutes to go out back and tour the bicycle. Let me show you. I've named her Blue."

Blue leaned on the shed near the large trash dump in the back of the school, but it looked like it belonged inside. Rusty and dented with a dangling chain, there was no rehabilitation that Angel could see. Blue wasn't blue at all, either; instead, the bike was the color of dry moss in a drought. All in all, Blue was a giant mess of an eyesore. Its three redeeming qualities were the third wheel, large basket on the rear, and sidecar for pulling a second passenger.

"Here she is!" said Miss Ferris as if Blue were a shiny new buggy. "Gorgeous, isn't it? I picked it off the side of the road last year. Who would simply abandon something like this? She could use a tiny bit of work, but imagine the possibilities, Angel. The books."

Angel bent forward to inspect the bicycle, and upon a closer look, she saw a tiny procession of spiders emerging from an intricate web on the rear basket. Angel leaped back in disgust; she loathed spiders with a terrified passion.

Miss Ferris noticed Angel's disgust and seemed cut by it. "She needs a bit of elbow grease, but between the three of us, we can have her shipshape in no time."

"So Isaiah's officially involved?"

"Oh, dear," she said. "He was involved, as you say, from the moment I explained it. Would you sacrifice the next few days to help get Blue in order? Sabbath off, of course."

"Miss Ferris," Angel said, attempting to sound calm. "This bike needs a lot of work."

"We can do it," she replied. "I swear we can."

Angel walked home that afternoon with a spring in her step. While she hadn't seen Isaiah after their morning talk, they'd be together a fair amount that summer. It'd be interesting to see him in that light—using his hands and mind and creativity to bring Blue back to life in order to hand out books.

It was exciting to think about—the three of them huddled together in such a small space, tackling a singular, and maybe insurmountable, goal as a team. It could only bring them closer. Also, Miss Ferris was a magnet to be around. Her student's lives improved when she was nearby.

Everybody knew everybody in Greenwood, but Miss Ferris was particularly popular. Daughter of the head deacon, and former college beauty queen. She could've gone anywhere, been anything, but instead, she moved back to inject love of culture and books into the youth of their district.

"Hey, Angel!" Deacon Yancey sat alone on his porch waving. It crossed Angel's mind that he may have been waiting for her to walk by all day just so he could have someone to talk to. She pushed in his gate to join him on the porch. "Can I get you another cup of tea?"

"Oh, no!" she replied too eagerly. "I mean, no thank you. I can't drink caffeine this late in the afternoon. It'll just keep me awake."

He jumped up from his porch swing anyway. "I've got herbal."

Before she could stop him, he disappeared back into his small home and began running the tap. Dreading that first sip, she slumped in her rocking chair. But then she saw him— Isaiah—walking quickly past the deacon's house. She felt her mouth turn up into a smile.

"Hey there!" she said, softly so Deacon Yancey wouldn't hear, but Isaiah only lowered his head in response.

She slowly let down her waving hand. She was no fool; he was ignoring her. As he walked onward, she decided not to care. There were too many wonderful things to come—a lucrative job being surrounded by books, and not to mention the Memorial Day parade on Monday. Isaiah was just a boy. A finicky one who'd been sucked into the delusions of W.E.B. Du Bois. Such foolishness, that! The test of time would show that Booker T. Washington's strategy was the superior one. Sure, there were undoubtedly flaws in Washington's argument, but it was the closest they had to real change in the entire community. Simple and easy to go down, it was.

Plow your own land. Pass along your methods to your children's children. Allow the white man to live in what he thinks is luxury while cultivating a valuable life alongside. A life akin to Greenwood. Fight not! Instead, focus on that we can control—ourselves. And one day, just like the tortoise, we shall pass the overzealous hare.

As the teakettle began to whistle from inside the house, Angel couldn't help feeling cut by Isaiah's snub. What could have happened between this morning and now? she wondered. Or the better question, *who* could've happened. Muggy, obviously. Angel made a point of hating no one, especially her contemporaries. High school was a tricky place, after all. A place of confusion and judgment. A place of endless searching for oneself but never quite finding the destination.

People did things they regretted in high school, her father had told her. Even he kicked himself from time to time about the smallest of slights he'd committed twenty years earlier. It was a cruel time, he'd said. He was absolutely correct, too. And since she'd been warned, she fought hard and strong to avoid the high school pitfall of being cruel. Sometimes, she thought, she took it too far in the opposite direction, becoming a bit of a pushover. An easy target. But Muggy seemed to find unbridled joy in making others' lives miserable.

Deacon Yancey burst through the screen door. "I think it's even better than the last time!" he said with such delight. Then he caught the sight of Isaiah turning the corner and frowned. "I'll never understand how idyllic Greenwood can produce such a boy. He's the worst of us. God cursed his sugary sweet mother with raising such a child all alone." He turned his attention to Angel. "She kind of reminds me of you."

Angel took a small sip and winced, this time at Deacon Yancey's harsh judgment, not the tea, which was horrible. She thought of Shakespeare. She wasn't necessarily Juliet, but Isaiah was definitely Romeo. A poet in wolf's clothing. A lover playing dress-up in order to fit in with Muggy. A covert reader was what he was, but it wasn't her place to take up for him. Everyone had to hold on to their own shovel, and decide whether to dig graves deep enough for themselves.

"Deacon," she started, trying to add a touch of nonchalance to her voice. "You seem to really not care for him. What has he done so horribly?"

Deacon Yancey jammed his feet to the porch floor to stop his swing from swaying. It was an action of pure hatred, which surprised Angel. Deacon Yancey, though old in his thoughts, was basically harmless. She'd never seen his face so twisted up in anger toward anyone.

"It'll take a minute to tell," he said with a scowl. "Long, long history of horrible in that family."

Again, Angel thought of Romeo, but not as the generic-lover-catchall Romeo. The Romeo that everyone despised for a valid reason. Romeo pre-Juliet—a dangerous prankster with a mean entourage and few redeeming qualities. Narcissistic Romeo. While that Romeo only gets a few opening pages in the play, Angel often thought of him. Rescued by love and beauty from a downward spiral of mischief. But why was every reader so quick to forget his misdeeds? So eager to give him a pass for being an awful human? The unwavering power of a hopeful love story, she thought. But not her and Deacon Yancey. They seemed to share a natural skepticism about such things.

Angel glanced at her watch. "I've got a little while before I have to be home." She blew on her tea and forced a large gulp. "What is it about Isaiah?"

Deacon Yancey released his feet and began swinging again.

"That dead daddy of his was always a troublemaker," he started.

Though his tone was harsh, Angel let out a brief sigh of relief. This had nothing at all to do with Isaiah. This was old foolishness of grudges held hard. She almost jumped up to leave, readying herself for an excuse to abandon Deacon Yancey. Maybe she'd blame baby Michael. Or her papa. Or even her mama. It wouldn't be a lie—she was sure that between the three of them, somebody needed her back home. She squirmed in her seat.

"Apple fell in the branches with Isaiah, though," he continued. "Remember my Pete? Never a bad bone in his body, Pete. Every father wants a son like that. A dream of a son, he is."

Angel wanted to show a tiny bit of interest before she left. "He's in Atlanta, right?"

Deacon Yancey nodded in response, staring off at the front gate. "Moved there soon as it happened."

Angel sat back again, intrigued, and took another sip of her tea. "What exactly happened?"

The story of Pete was a convoluted one around town. His legend loomed large within the surrounding cities. Supposedly, he was voted most handsome, most likely to succeed, most popular, all of it. The rumors were that he'd been excelling at absolutely everything.

But the day after graduation from one of the schools a few counties over, he'd left Oklahoma and never returned, not even for his mother's funeral. It was as if he'd vanished into thin air. Angel had known more than most about this since they'd all graduated high school together—her mother, father, even Isaiah's parents were in his large graduating class.

Angel realized Deacon Yancey hadn't answered her. "You don't have to tell me, Deacon, I understand."

He looked over at her like someone stuck a flaming dagger in his heart. "I haven't told a soul about my boy," he said slowly. "Promised my wife I never would do."

"I don't understand, Deacon."

"That daddy of his lied on my Pete. Told a gang of white men Pete had stolen some tiny piece of something from their grocery. Pete had no reason to steal. More too, he had better sense than to take from the white man. But that ole daddy of his got my Pete beat so bad he never was the same. His mama neither. She'd been dying long before that bitter cold day last September."

ISAIAH

A coward. A follower. A stupid, stupid idiot for leaving his journal on the bed. For trusting entirely untrustworthy Dorothy Mae. Isaiah hated himself.

Angel had been talking to Deacon Yancey again, too. Things were definitely not looking good for him. Deacon Yancey had disliked him since the day he entered the world, his mother had told him when he was very young. She wouldn't go into deep detail as to why, but she did say that Isaiah was a firm representation of his only son Pete's failure. Isaiah's precious mother was supposed to marry Pete. After a decade of puppy love, Isaiah's mother met his father. And that was the end of that. According to Greenwood's vines, she snuck out the back door of her house, leaving Pete on her front porch holding a bouquet of verbena.

In that moment, Isaiah realized just how many verbena had opened toward the sun, happy and healthy. In the spring, Greenwood was overrun with them. So much so, Westerners traveled from all over Oklahoma for photographs. Inspired to write, he sat on a neighbor's front stoop and removed the journal from his bag.

Fingers itching, he began a stream-of-consciousness poem to the flowers surrounding him.

For the Greenwood Verbena

I'm Confused
But don't you be.
Bathe in the light.
I cannot quite see.
It's large for you.
And small for me.
Don't give up on love.
You're Confused.
But nothing like me.
I'm trapped in the deep dark.
You're wild and free.
You do you,
And I'll do me.
But don't give up on love.

Then, all of a sudden, the pages of his journal flipped forward so forcefully they knocked his pen to the fertile ground. Fingering through, there was a thick gap in the fanning of the pages. Fringy wisps springing forward from the inner spine, missing pages. He recognized which immediately—the perfectly passionate college letters of intent to Morehouse and Howard.

A wave of hatred overtook the entirety of his body, heat radiating from his trembling fingers. A knot in his stomach released itself; he was no longer afraid. Now, dear Lord, he was enraged. The instant that he realized his intent letters were missing, he no longer dared to care about Greenwood hierarchy and where he fit in it. Muggy had ripped out a chess piece in his long game. Popularity didn't stand up to that challenge.

Morehouse would mold him into a man of maroon and white. A big-city fighter feeding poetry and power into the pipeline of Atlanta, where Du Bois lived and, therefore, would certainly take notice.

Or Howard. Equally statured and skillfully placed in the center of the nation's capital for maximum political impact. He could stand tall on flipped milk crates reciting words into the receptive minds ready for social change.

But trickster Muggy. Small-town Muggy. Muggy with no hope for anything more had stolen a chess piece off of his board.

Surely he could write more letters. Writing was, after all, his forte. But that wasn't nearly the point. Taken words crossed a line that Isaiah hadn't realized existed. Not only taken words, but a taken future. Taken escape from the place where every single one of the thirty-five blocks reminded him of his father.

Glancing through angry, squinted eyes, he saw Mrs. Turner's tiny flower shop, where his father would buy his mother a single yellow rose every Friday evening for no reason at all. A bit farther in the distance, he spotted the ticking clock towering over Mr. Massey's dry cleaners, who crisped his father's shirt exactly the way he liked them. And then, looking down at his own feet, he realized he'd taken a seat on the porch in front of the very walkway where his father had taught him to ride a two-wheeled bike.

A burning overtook Isaiah's nose, and he began to cry. Not a blubbering, but a fuming. Like a teased bull in a ring—surrounded by spectators dressed to witness shame. Like a boar shot to suffer. Like Du Bois.

Isaiah had been a prankster at best. A coward. A follower. A stupid, stupid idiot. But deep down on the inside, he was plotting. Secretly and satisfyingly carving an escape hatch for himself. A path to greatness—leadership. And now Muggy Little Jr. threatened it.

He stood to his feet and headed straight to Muggy's house. He had three blocks to stretch and squeeze his fists. He was about to beat his best friend's ass once and for all.

When he reached Muggy's home, he saw his grinning eye peek through the front blind. Isaiah got to banging on the glass, shamelessly loud and chaotic. Obviously at the end of his lengthy rope, Isaiah was released from his cage.

"Open the door, Muggy!" he yelled in a crazed slur. "Come out and face me like a man!"

But Muggy didn't come.

"Coward!" Isaiah yelled from the center of Muggy Little Jr.'s front yard. "Coward!"

ANGEL

A dusting came over Greenwood. Brown swirls of road rose knee-high, teasing at Angel's senses. Long-settled dirt lifted from the curve of the train track with strange beauty. As she felt herself out of Deacon Yancey's sights, Angel sat on a patchy spot of grass near the track's edge to take in the look of the quaint town she loved.

Greenwood. "Negro Wall Street" as Booker T. Washington named it. Appropriate, she thought. No better name for such an active place of Black excellence. A few summers ago, when her papa still tilted his hats just so, they'd taken the train to visit family in Florida. Her father told her to prepare herself for a different perspective on Black life. A rougher view, he'd called it. But when they arrived, she was not prepared.

Stepping off the train, she was greeted by a large-breasted

woman with a face shaped like the moon. Her own face buried in bosom, Angel smelled the crust of peach pie in her grandmother's chest. The aroma of love shown through freshly picked fruits baked into desserts. Sitting there in the Greenwood grass, Angel could nearly smell it. She closed her eyes for a brief moment and smiled, but the memory was replaced by the rest of her grandmother's tiny Florida town.

Dust. Not too different from the very dust surrounding her own town, but the similarity ended there. In Florida, the dirt was sinister. "Red from the spilt blood of our ancestors," her father had told her to her mother's chagrin. "Too much, Robert," her mother had said with an elbow to his ribs. "You'll scare her to death."

Angel wasn't scared at all, though. She was instead curious. When her papa's mother finally released her, Angel took in the line of shotgun houses. Aproned women went about their business, in and out of their creaking homes, and Angel wondered why they looked so sad. Suspendered men also trudged along with invisible weight hunching their shoulders toward the ground. Children ran through the red dirt, toeing squares into the dust to make hopscotch. The game was to reach the end of the hopscotch before a gust took the lines away and no one could make it in time to win.

As the train left, Angel noticed the small white side of town just on the other side. So close a well-armed pitcher could break one of their windows from where she'd stood. She saw white women cross-stitching patterns in lazy rocking chairs as Black ladies chased their wild children. She saw white men managing broad-shouldered, sweaty Black men to do their hard work in the distance. She saw the very opposite of Greenwood. Her papa was right to warn her.

Now, as the sun began setting to orange, Angel peeled herself from the ground and began to walk home. She thought much about what Deacon Yancey had told her of Isaiah's father.

Enormous secrets of a small town could create a rot on the inside. And eventually, that sick spot spread to other places like bad fruit in a basket. For the deacon, it spread to Isaiah without a single doubt. The deacon despised Isaiah as a placeholder for his dead father; that much was obvious. But such secrets shouldn't be secrets, Angel thought.

Deacon Yancey said that there was no one else left alive that knew the truth about Pete. He was the only one carrying around such a load. His wife knew, of course, but she'd gone on to leave him with it. Then, on the last dusty day of the school year, Deacon Yancey decided to share it with Angel.

She wanted to give Deacon Yancey the benefit of the doubt. She wanted to believe he told her as a warning about Isaiah. As a loving church member would. She, however, knew the deacon, selfish and lonely, only wanted to give away a portion of his burden so he didn't have to carry it all.

Angel wanted to help people, but she also wanted to live a life of her own. Without ghosts and vendettas dropped onto her like blinding raindrops. But now, she had no choice. She was carrying it right along with him, and approaching her home, she swore she'd never share that secret's burden. Not even with Isaiah.

Michael had to be asleep, because her street was quiet. Making her way onto her cool porch, she pushed the door in to find her precious papa snoring on the couch. He'd already been wiped up and changed by her mother, who was likely exhausted from all that solo work. Guilt took ahold. Not because her mother had done it herself, but because of the relief she felt from not having to help. That'd been the first evening in weeks she'd be able to lay herself down as soon as she walked in the door. She crawled into her bed and fell asleep in her school clothes.

ANGEL

"Wake up, sleepy," her mother called out. "First day of summer break. You know what that means."

Angel wiped at her eyes and smiled. Lemon pancakes was what it meant, ever since she was small. Another school year done, her favorite breakfast as a reward.

Dragging herself out of bed, she made her way to the kitchen to find no one in there.

"We're in the front room," her mother said with less zeal. "Join us."

Her mother had pushed up a square folding table as close to her papa as possible, likely to catch his dropped food. His untouched pancakes were steaming in front of his weakly smiling eyes. Angel could tell he wanted to lift his hand to greet her but couldn't. He was failing fast.

"Papa!" Her phony exuberance briefly lifted a cloud from his tired eyes. "And thank you, Mama."

Angel pulled her own plate to the smallest angle of the folding table to give her father as much room as possible. Her mama had done the same, respectfully leaving him the head and two sides. A lion of a man, he'd always deserved such deference. And even now, fighting for life or clamoring for death, they would provide him this long-earned esteem.

"I have news," Angel announced, eyeing the fluffy holes in her pancakes to avoid looking at her papa's, in such a pitiful state. "Miss Ferris has asked me and a young man named Isaiah down the street to hand out books for a little extra money this summer."

An unreadable silence held on too long, so Angel decided, nervously, to fill it.

"She says there are still rough blocks down the way in Greenwood. They mostly keep to themselves over there, I think, because I only see them at Mount Zion on Easter and Christmas Sundays."

She felt her parents stiffen as she spoke. She stuffed a mouthful of pancakes and began speaking again before they were swallowed.

"Reading is fundamental is what the teachers have been telling us since we started school. We're riding around on an old bike with a sidecar attached. Never seen anything quite like that. Has to be cleaned up and repaired. I was hoping Mr. Morris felt quite up to sturdying the wooden pieces and then picking up heavy-duty polish from old Mr. Odom's hardware store down by the barbershop on the Avenue. Poor contraption's rustier than anything."

When she was done talking, she gave in to the silence, fully expecting a firm no from both of them. Studying her plate, she'd only taken one pie-slice-shaped hunk from her stack, but she was no longer hungry. Selfishly, she'd wanted out of this house for a few hours every day. Summer meant no escape from Michael, Mama's braiding, and, most of all, her now-pitiful papa.

Last summer, he was the strongest of them. Lifting her into too-tight hugs and twirling her mama into dipped-down kisses. Working from sunup to sundown and still coming home hopeful and happy and eager to help—tired but grinning like he'd rather be doing nothing else in the world. He brought the sunshine then. He only brought gray clouds with him now.

"I'm sorry," Angel said aloud but really to her selfish self.

"Isaiah," her mother said simply. "Certainly not my first choice."

Then Angel repeated a little lower, "I'm sorry."

"But," her mother continued, "a worthy cause, nonetheless. What do you think?" she asked Papa.

He could only get out two words. "Worthy . . . cause." And then he began breathing with much effort.

She couldn't believe it, she thought, making her way to Miss Ferris's house, which was three and a half blocks away.

Her first paying job. And helping people. The rest wasn't important. Not really.

"The rest isn't important," she told herself aloud as she pushed through Miss Ferris's backyard gate to see that Isaiah had already arrived.

ISAIAH

There was no air left in Greenwood. No. There was only Angel coming toward him. A hush came as she approached, slowly, carefully. Curiously? What was that expression on her face? He had to admit he didn't know her well enough to perfectly place that look. Apprehension, he thought. Of him, surely. Half-witted him, who'd dared to over-look such a girl for so many years. Actually, apprehension and caution. Yes. She moved toward him as she would an unstuck grenade. He was that, but not in the ways she seemed to think.

Pried free from Muggy, he was no longer a terrifying thing. Now he would do whatever she asked of him. Be who she wanted him to be. Behave in ways she longed for a man to behave. With Muggy, he was mean. Uncharacteristically so, and with no real rhyme or reason. With Angel, he assumed, he would be better, kinder, more empathetic. But without either, Isaiah was floating along with no leader to lead him. Secretly terrified to lead his own self.

"Hi," she said to him, face still frozen with watchfulness.

He said nothing in return. Not even as much as a hi. He wondered when he had become the dumbest of Doras.

"Hi, Miss Ferris," she said. "What's the plan?"

"I'm headed to pick up a few supplies from Mr. Odom's," she replied before hoisting a bag onto her shoulder. "You two, head on inside and pick the first batch of books. You'll need ten or so. You choose five," she told Isaiah. "And you choose five," she then told Angel.

"What's our age group?" Angel's words freed from the bow of her lips with such grace. "How young are we talking here?"

"Good question," Isaiah said, nodding along like a parroting idiot.

Miss Ferris chuckled knowingly. "Toddler on up. I'll be back in a bit."

With one last wink at Isaiah, she whistled away.

"Hope she has a copy of *The Souls of Black Folk*." Isaiah smiled as wide as he ever had, anticipating Angel being impressed by his obvious passion and love for the greatest man who ever lived.

He expected her to stop in her tracks, look back at him, and fall into a heap. Instead, she walked ahead into Miss Ferris's home library as if she hadn't heard him. Surely, she hadn't heard him.

The library, organized alphabetically with much care, was small but stunning. The slight room just off the kitchen was likely meant for laundering. Miss Ferris, however, had installed ceiling-high shelving and two overlarge chairs that shared a tiny table and quaint lamp. A poet's paradise, Isaiah thought.

"Wow," Angel said.

"Yeah," Isaiah said. "Oh! There it is."

He eased an immaculate hardcover copy of *The Souls of Black Folk* from the shelf and held it in Angel's sight lines so she had to see. Surely now she'd be rapt.

She shouldered past his raised book and lifted an equally pristine copy of *Up from Slavery*.

Isaiah felt his eyes double in size. She really was a Washington follower, just like his mother. Like he himself had been prior to Librarian Edith liberating his thinking.

A light went off inside of him, brightening his voice and heart and body. A knowing filled him up—he needed to unshackle this angel. Release her from the passive teachings of a dead man, rest his soul, and introduce her to the unfettered future of their people. Everywhere would be Greenwood. Every Black neighborhood in the world would recycle its own dollar until it went out of print. Every Black man would stand at the front stoop of his own tidy home, arms folded, cigar lit, hat tilted, daring the jealous-hearted white man to try him. Every Black woman would nurse her own baby safely in her own home, stroking its tiny head while rocking in her own rocking chair. That was the way of the future, and Isaiah

Wilson was about to introduce this gorgeous, if not naive, angel to the new Negro way.

"I see it now," he said with a slight, automatic click of the heels. "I'm here to save you."

ANGEL

"Say that again," she replied with disgusted shock. "I heard you incorrectly, surely."

"I'm here," he repeated with even more excitement than the first time, "to save you from yourself. Can't you see it? You're stuck, and I'm going to pull you out."

Angel could think of absolutely nothing kind to say in response to such insolence. How dare he? This was the twenties, after all. Many women worked outside the home while their husbands were away. All had minds to think for themselves without arrogant, haughty, know-everything boys telling them how to think. Pull her out from what exactly? Save *her*? He dared.

"You, Isaiah Wilson, will not save me from one thing, you hear me?" she replied with uncontrolled, flailing parts. As a dancer, she could feel her body in ways non-dancers could not. She knew what the lift of an arm meant versus the flick of a neck. Or straightening of stature versus slouching of the same. With that knowledge, she utilized her body to speak on her behalf. But something about Isaiah Wilson made her forget.

"You . . . ," he started. "You don't understand."

"I should save *you* from your relentless mistreatment of those who don't deserve it. Your needless meanness. Your . . . your . . . your . . . oppression."

She felt breathless, her chest rising and falling with anger she rarely let boil to the surface. But there was no holding back with him. Something about this boy made her absolutely loosed.

"I—" he started, palms in the air as if surrendering in battle.

"You, nothing," she interrupted. "You, Isaiah Wilson, nothing!"

His head bowed forward like a caught dog as he replaced the book he'd been so excited about on the shelf.

"And you know what else?" she asked. "Du Bois is just like you, a tyrant. A strongheaded brute of a man, elbowing his way to the front of the line without taking into account life as it is. I've seen how our people live outside of Greenwood. I've seen the heavy weight of generations on the backs of our folks. There's a mentality, Isaiah. One of downness, you understand? One of being pushed so far down that there's no way up. Greenwood is a rarity, a bright spot in the wide world of darkness." She folded her arms. "Let me dare guess, you've never been outside of this place?"

Head still bowed, he asked, "Can I speak?"

"Well, I asked you a question, didn't I?"

"No, I have not been outside of Greenwood."

"Ha!" she said in response. "Well then, you should."

A few tense moments passed.

"Can I speak again now?" he asked.

Angel nodded.

"I've never been outside of this place," he said with a sadness all over him that suddenly made Angel sad, too. Was she being too harsh on him? "But I devour books about those places. My father used to get the Negro papers sent up. I still have them if you want to ever see. I know our people are in a state of terror. I know and I long for a shifting. Sometimes, when Muggy's off somewhere with his parents, I sit and watch the white folks go on about their business on the other side of the tracks. I see them, too. Breezing through as our women do the hard work of their households. Shopping for the lovely things as our women shop for their groceries. Holding only their pocketbooks as our women hold their babies. It's sickening. It needs to change. I'd like to have a part in that change. And, in my opinion"—he bowed his head deeper before finishing his thought—"Booker T. will only keep us where we were. Maybe, just maybe, a bully like Du Bois is what we need."

Angel thought for a moment and decided . . .

"No," she said sternly before paging through *Up from Slavery* to find her favorite passage. "Ah, listen to this part. '*The very fact that the white boy is conscious that, if he fails in life, he will disgrace the whole family record, extending back through many generations, is of—*'"

"'*Tremendous value in helping him to resist temptations.*'" Isaiah seemingly couldn't help himself. "I memorized nearly the entire book. Ask me anything."

"You seem quite proud of this," she replied, trying her best not to look impressed, though she absolutely was. "Go on, then."

As if he'd been given permission to take center stage, he dramatically lifted his arms, feigning Booker T. Washington. "'*The fact that the individual has behind and surrounding him proud family history and connection serves as a stimulus to help him to overcome obstacles when striving for success,*'" Isaiah said in a single breath. "Is that enough? Or should I go on? I'm more than happy to—"

"What does it mean?" Angel was the one interrupting this time.

"It's obvious what it means, I'd say," he started. "Born enslaved and to a white father, he longs for the life of that white boy. An easier road toward his selfish desires. On the surface, Washington was driven by ambition to better his people. I believed that, too, at first. But actually, it's quite the opposite; he was an Uncle Tom."

"Don't you dare say that about him!" Angel hissed as soon as the two words came through his lips. "He was no Uncle Tom, but of course you'd think that of him." She turned her back to Isaiah.

He softened his voice to respond, realizing he'd over-stepped some invisible line. "Could you help me understand what you think, then?"

Angel considered it for a moment and then decided he was right. She couldn't allow him to drag the name of Booker T. Washington through the mud. Besides, he'd vocalized, passionately so, his zeal for Du Bois. It was due time she'd done the same for her own personal hero.

She sunk into one of the overstuffed armchairs and began to explain her position. Not passionately with wild arms and stomping feet like Isaiah had, but calmly, with much care. She held *Up from Slavery* in the air.

"This is no book. Not in the same way Du Bois presents a book, it's not. This is a diary—both extremely personal and woefully terrifying in its raw honesty. Washington presents the world as it existed for a boy born property to a mother likely taken against her will." She leaned toward Isaiah, who was now sitting across from her, rapt. "No boy should have to know such evil exists so early in life. Or worse, be descended from it.

"As he writes these words, he is a man, yes, but still a boy," she said, pausing to carefully place her index finger onto Isaiah's chest. "In here, Washington is still just born. Trapped in a log cabin with a too-small door and no knowledge of the importance of a toothbrush nor bedsheets. He's an intellectual who cannot read. Working hard labor with his ill-equipped, soft hands. Isaiah, he's a man willing to admit the frequency of his tears to the world with no holds barred.

"The lines of this book should not be memorized verbatim." She paused to smile affectionately at the work. "They should not be bragged about in desirable company," she said, still smiling but no longer with her eyes. "To adequately understand these lines, one must read between them."

Isaiah took a moment and then raised his hand as if he were in class. When she nodded, he continued, ready for debate. "Why, in your opinion, then, does he so easily forgive the cruelty of the white men? For that matter, his own father, who never staked claim to him. He even went on to discuss the great kindness of so-called masters and mistresses and how those kindnesses are to be revered by all. When these are the same evildoers oppressing our people. Beating us. Ravaging our women. Stealing our children. Burning our homes to the rocky ground."

Angel leaned in even closer. Fully accepting and appreciating the opportunity to explain what she knew and he only thought he knew. "But don't you see, Isaiah? He has not forgiven anything at all. Not one iota has he absolved. That's merely the false bluster of the angriest man that possibly ever lived. In regard to the great kindness of mistresses and masters, as you say, if you read on, you'll see that he references many men who stayed in bondage even though they were given the freedom they'd long desired. He's angry at them, too. So angry, in fact, that he walks away from his job in the stable salt mines, penniless and starving, to create a path for himself and, as you call us, our people.

"If you take this text literally," she said, with compassion toward a boy who clearly did not understand men, "you will undoubtedly believe Booker to be nothing more than an Uncle You-Know-What-I-Dare-Not-Say. But if you instead take into account the life of the man, the whole of his life, you will never again defame him."

She leaned back, sinking deeper into the softness of the chair.

Isaiah, so eager to debate just a moment ago, could formulate no adequate response.

ISAIAH

Argument turned to banter as Isaiah and Angel attempted to choose the other eight of their book selections. They'd devised a game of sorts where one called out a favorite title and the other dramatically struck it down like a referee would a foul ball.

"*The Secret Garden*," Angel said as if she were speaking of a precious newborn puppy dog. "Please don't strike this one. It's a beautiful book, I swear this."

Isaiah rose his arms high up in the air, ready to strike. She looked up at him like a doe would its mother. "Please," she repeated. "Let me have this one, Isaiah, please."

He loved the way she said his name. This girl sure could truly look pitiful when she wanted to, Isaiah thought. And entirely beautiful. Too beautiful to be real. He nearly reached out his hand to touch her face just to check. He could've sworn tears were welling up in the bottom rims of her large eyes, eyes that shined with yearning. Dear God, if she looked at him with such eyes every day . . . He couldn't dream of such fortune.

"Okay," he gave in. "Though it's against my very instinct, you may have *The Secret Garden.*"

"Ha!" she shouted before leaping into the air. "You're easy to fleece, aren't you?"

He wanted to throw his arms around her waist and kiss her. She was everything he wanted. More than that. She was, in every sense, a Black angel of his dreams.

"I got you." She nudged him.

"You got me," he replied, not nearly angry.

"Ooh." She leaped again. "*Peter and Wendy.*" Pushing her luck this time.

High up on her toes, just like when she danced, she reached for the light green copy of *Peter and Wendy* stuck between a squatty line of Beatrix Potter books and the script for *Phaedra* on the topmost shelf. She couldn't quite reach, which Isaiah saw as an opportunity.

He shifted toward her, falling into a move he'd utilized on countless girls before. Then he shook the sly off of himself like he would a buzzing fly. He became himself, or tried to anyway. Calm down, Isaiah, she's just as human as you are after all, he told himself. Step forward, get the book, bring it down to her, and step back again. So he did.

Calculating, he first looked down at his right foot and stepped it forward long enough to cover the remaining distance between them—one and a half feet approximately. And then he brought the other forward to meet it. Next, careful not to brush against her in any way, he lifted his left arm over her braided hair and easily grasped the book. Okay, he thought. So far, so good.

But then she looked over at him with those eyes again. Those dangerous eyes, still filled with shining lights and his own reflection. They were close. Close enough to find a sneaky gray eyelash curling along with the rest of them. Close enough to see that her eyebrows were not nearly the same. Actually, one was wild at the inner corners and the other was slicked down and behaved. Her mismatched eyebrows alone could take up two whole pages in his journal. He was close enough to catch sight of a single curl poking out from one of her braids.

"I'm back." Miss Ferris burst into the back door with the supplies, startling Isaiah.

His arm jerked forward into the meticulously organized bookshelves, sending the entire top row of Beatrix Potter onto Angel's perfect head.

"I'm so sorry," he said, patting at her cheek like the idiot he was. "Are you okay? You got the whole Beatrix Potter collection head-on." So stupid, stupid, stupid.

She grinned before squatting down to pick them up. "At least they weren't the full-sized ones, though."

"No," he said, cowering next to her. "I'll get them. I can do this. I've got this; I swear I do."

Isaiah felt droplets of sweat collecting at his chin and armpits. Frazzled was an understatement. He was a mess.

"Isaiah." He'd forgotten Miss Ferris was even standing there to witness his fumbling. "Come help me with the bag. Angel can join us after she's gathered the rabbits."

Miss Ferris had given him a much-needed way out. As soon as he was out of eyeshot, Isaiah's palms floated to cover his face. Miss Ferris placed her concerned hand on his back and said, "Come on."

After some hesitation, he followed her through the entire house. Around the pantry, stocked with a floor-to-ceiling wall of home-canned peaches, plums, and apples. Under the wooden staircase and through a far side door he had to duck down to get under. He was thankful for the distance.

"What is wrong with me?" he said before becoming a heap on the sitting room couch. "Something's terribly wrong with me."

"You know."

That's what he loved most about Miss Ferris. She wasn't the type to labor him with lengthy speeches and advice. Instead, she allowed the words to come to him as they willed. Besides, he did know. The blundering. The planning of steps and movements. The unsteadiness of thoughts and mind and body. All of this was love. He'd read enough books to know that.

"Do you need to write?" She finally asked the perfectly correct question.

"I do."

"Pen's over there," she said as she ducked out of the room. "Join us when you're finished. I feel certain this will be a magical poem."

The jacket of his journal was moist with the sweat of stress and his pen nearly dull. Preferring his own writing utensil, he carefully bit tiny pieces of wood from the tip to reveal more lead. Overwhelmed, he couldn't bring himself to write a word about Angel. Knowing he'd have to face her again soon, he didn't want to stir too much more emotion to the raw surface.

He thought instead of the way she'd spoken of Booker T. Washington. Such reverence for a man Isaiah knew to be undeserving. Such selflessness toward a man who only spoke of himself and his accomplishments. Poor Angel, ankle-deep in Washington's muck. Hypnotized by his tragic beginnings and circumstance, never acknowledging his arrogance, feebleness, and lack of will to stand against his oppressor. A fine speaker with no backbone to speak of. And Angel, ignorant of the workings of the world with no desire to be educated. Anyone else, he would've written off; her, he wanted to save.

> ### Booker (for Angel)
> *Born bonded in bondage,*
> *Billowed and bandaged,*
> *Beaten by bastards,*
> *In bally brimmed hats.*

Fledgling and crying,
As kinfolk lay dying,
Still he praised his butchers,
Don't dare justify that.
Up from Slavery, he bolstered,
Bragged of full civilized meals,
While white men holstered their hostlers,
With loaded prepared steel.
To shoot down his dear kindred,
And ravage his descended,
But don't blame the white man,
He said, the white man was kind.
No excuses, my Angel,
Not for abuses so major.
No admissions, no bias, or Biblical
*   effervescence,*
Just submission, compliance and pitiful
*   acquiescence.*
Deserve your deference, he does not,
Nor benefit of the doubt,
Not your reverence,
He was mere denigrate, speeches for aught.
All dialogue without action,
Hasty tongue with no roar,
Only idioms, vernaculars,
Spoken language of strong men who
*   welcomed war.*

Now for Angel,
I say,
So sorry to break your precious heart,
But your love for Booker Washington
  isn't smart.

As he read the poem back to himself, a heavy weight lifted from Isaiah's body. Writing was a spewing of corrupted energy for him, clearing the path for the calm decency he longed for within himself. Even flawed or misused, his words strung together in rhythmic clumps, separated by spaces giving them the look of Claude McKay or James Weldon Johnson. The act of writing brought him back to where he was supposed to be. There was no Muggy in that place. No enslaved heroes. No premature death of a parent. Not even Angel was there. In the space after, Isaiah made words work as one in perfect concert, Isaiah found only himself. He could breathe.

Airways clear, he picked himself up and snaked his way back through Miss Ferris's bookish, artistic home, noticing things he hadn't before. Most walls in her home had been covered with shelving to house a world of books. Tucked in horizontally, diagonally, and every way they'd stay, books overwhelmed the place. For anyone else it would've been hoarding, but for her, it was quaint. The stocked pantry was the only area Isaiah observed without a single book inside.

Fascinated by such a meticulous cold room, Isaiah stopped in to further inspect it. Mason jars of segregated dried beans lined the walls—white beans with whites, speckled darks with speckled, black with blacks. Air-sealed peaches, plums, figs, and apples made up the opposite side of the pantry's walls. In the center, handmade breads with large craters splitting the center were stuffed in handled baskets lining multiple shelves.

Isaiah breathed in Miss Ferris's untainted personal space, where she could be whoever she wanted to be—teacher, baker, gardener, a free woman. Such a small thing, the ability to be oneself, but so forbidden to so many of his people, even now. Every Black woman should be able to live in such calm creativity if she so pleased. One thing his angel reminded him to see: Greenwood was unique in that way.

Again, he took in a deep breath. The room smelled of the best sort of home: old-world, delicious freedom. So many would never be able to breathe in such an intangible thing as freedom. Why him? Why Miss Ferris? Why Angel? None of this was fair, but fairness was of no import.

"Observing my spoils, I see." Miss Ferris startled him.

"I'm sorry," he replied, heading for the doorway. "It's just . . ." He considered sharing his thoughts with her. "I'm sure this was a lot of work."

Angel's large, impressed eyes peeked over Miss Ferris's left shoulder. "You did all this yourself?"

"I did," Miss Ferris said before angling her body to let Angel inside the pantry door. "I don't think of this as work, though. This belongs to me. I planted it, grew it, picked it, and will soon eat it. My mother would've died for such an opportunity to work for her own pickings. Her mother, too. Working for one's own benefit is not working at all."

Isaiah took this as an opening. "Actually," he said, "that's why I came in here. The look of it, the care, it's sovereignty. This doesn't exist anywhere else in the world for Blacks." He looked into Angel's confused face. "I know this may sound stagey, forgive me, but our people don't get to have this life. What's so special about the three of us that we do?"

"Follow me into the kitchen," Miss Ferris said without answering. "I'd say it's time for lunch; red soup and corn bread. Every ingredient specially pulled from this very pantry."

Following close behind Miss Ferris, Angel whispered to Isaiah, "I find myself feeling the same thing every time I pass so many Black-owned businesses in Deep Greenwood. I can't quite press my finger on it. The closest word I can think of is guilt."

"Yes," he said as if she'd identified the word his mind had been dancing around without catching ahold of it. "Guilt. As unfounded as it may be, that's what's tugging my insides."

"Have a seat, you two," Miss Ferris said before pouring two warm bowls of aromatic soup over generous squares of dark corn bread.

ANGEL

Angel was surprised by the scrumptiousness of her first slurp of red soup. It was nearly shocking to her palate. She searched the bowl for a valid reason why this basic red soup should taste so incredible, but only found pole snap beans, scraped corn, and floating bits of tomato. There was no rhyme or reason. Angel decided to close her eyes and enjoy it.

"My Lord, Miss Ferris," Isaiah blurted out. "What did you do to this soup? It's the best I've ever had."

Angel laughed and thanked him internally for asking.

"The trick is the roux," Miss Ferris replied. "And, dear boy, I have no idea how to tell you. A roux is a feeling more than it is a method. You just pour, stir, poke, prod, sniff, then ready. My mama's mama taught me."

"I'd love to watch you make it someday," Angel said with much apprehension. Some women took it as an affront, asking for secret family recipes and tricks in the kitchen, but Angel couldn't help herself. "If you'll have me."

At first, Miss Ferris looked taken aback; then she softened. "That's a dangerous question to ask a woman, you do know that."

"I do know that."

"I admire your courage," Miss Ferris joked. "I'd love to show you my roux. Both of you, if you'd like." They nodded with full mouths. "We should dissect this guilt you're both feeling," Miss Ferris said. "Since you're eating, and enjoying, I'll begin."

Miss Ferris wiped her hands on the same checkerboard kitchen rag Angel's mother had hanging over her stove back home, and settled into a dining chair across from them. Every Greenwood household likely had the same rag, Angel imagined. She remembered stacks of them on display in Mr. Odom's hardware store window. She recalled that stack shrinking every time she'd passed by. That was one of Angel's favorite things about living in a town such as Greenwood.

"First of all, I feel it, too," said Miss Ferris as she clasped her hands and rested her chin on them. "I believe with my whole heart that every Black person living, even those still living under the foot of the white man, feels some small inkling of this. Our people have been fractured, you see? Strategically separated into classes within itself. Angel, you know the passage in *Up from Slavery* when Booker T. Washington discussed those who went back into bondage? With grinning faces and peppy steps, they housed themselves comfortably underneath the white man's foot. Why would they do this?"

Angel took a moment to consider. This portion of Washington's book was much criticized in her world. Broken into pieces and reasons to call her hero an Uncle You-Know-What. Every fabric of her wanted to defend him, especially in the company of her much-beloved teacher and a Du Bois worshipper like Isaiah.

"I . . . ," she started, then stopped.

How could she offer an explanation? She, sixteen years old and female, would run as fast and far as she could away from such nightmares. Children taken from the arms of their mothers, mothers razed by filthy men, men emasculated by generations of forced submission. All the compassion in the world couldn't explain that. But she couldn't dare say that in such company.

"I have trouble vindicating this passage," she said simply. "I have no words."

"Ha!" Isaiah shouted, boasting his position. This single, conceited syllable made Angel's blood boil. "See!"

Angel had nearly lost sight of the dreadfulness of him, but there it was on full display. So blinded by his own will and cause that no one else's mattered. "You truly only think of your winning, don't you? No one else exists in the world if you win an argument?"

Just seeing he'd offended her, he cowered. "I wasn't thinking just then . . ."

"That's right, you weren't thinking," she snapped her reply. "You're no better than the pastor cherry-picking sermons to justify his own failures. No better than Muggy. And you know what? No better than the master-minded white man, winning by any means necessary."

She knew it was too far before she'd said it. She also knew he was nothing like the white man, but in that very moment, she only cared to hurt him as much as he'd hurt her. And when she finally caught his gaze, she realized that she had done what she set out to do.

"Angel," Miss Ferris interjected firmly. "Never demean a Black man in such a way, you hear me? No matter how angry he makes you, you never compare a good man to such another. Look at me in my eyes, Angel, or you will never be welcomed in my home again."

Angel didn't want to look up. Shame weighed down on the back of her neck, and she just wanted to disappear under the table, never to emerge again. She'd crossed the line. Tears burned the bottom rims of her eyes, and an itch came over her now-running nose. The pit of her stomach fell as far down as it would go, but she knew she had to look up. So she did. Locking disappointed eyes with Miss Ferris made Angel cry freely.

"Never . . ." Miss Ferris forced her words through fenced teeth. "Never tell a good Black man he's just like the evilest white one. None deserve to be trapped with cruel captors, rapists, murderers. Especially not by a Black woman. Do you understand me?" Angel nodded in response, but that wasn't enough. "Speak your understanding aloud."

"I understand." She blubbered fractured syllables to make up the words and then turned to Isaiah, whose eyes were also filled with tears. "I'm sorry. I didn't mean it at all."

"I know," he replied, trying to smile and failing. "I shouldn't have mocked you, either."

"You really should take care with that, Isaiah," Miss Ferris told him, voice and face now calmed. "Or else you'll make yourself look like a know-it-all who knows very little indeed. Now, about that difficult passage in *Up from Slavery*."

"We don't have to—" Isaiah said.

"We most certainly do," Miss Ferris interrupted. "Listen, both of you. The author of the work is creating contention between you, I see that, but leave that out of this discussion for a moment. The question is why would an otherwise-capable man stay in bondage when he has a choice to leave it? My answer, no matter how hypothesized, is incomparable, unexplainable, unfathomable terror. Such terror should not exist in the God-fearing world, but it does.

"We all get one life to live. One chance to make something beautiful of ourselves or to not, that's what we know to be true here in Greenwood. That's the difference between us and them, nothing else. We are no better on the inside. We simply know a Black life can be transformed from that of servitude to that of unmatched intelligence, resourcefulness, creativity, triumph." She paused to wipe at her eyes.

"That's the guilt we're feeling on the inside. It has nothing at all to do with the ability to plant and sow vegetables, or own thriving businesses, or even walk down the street without harassment. It's the immaterial knowledge that we, Black people, can be even better than whites if we want to be. And furthermore, much to their dismay, we don't need them to survive. Everyone should possess this knowledge, but the men who stayed in bondage didn't."

Thoughtful silence came over the kitchen, and pain crept in with it. No one won the Booker T. Washington versus W.E.B. Du Bois argument in that moment. Truth itself won. Truth that neither stolen innocence nor property outweighed stolen esteem for one's own capabilities. That was the true travesty of slavery and, furthermore, the true triumph of Greenwood.

"We deserve to be here, though, right?" Isaiah asked Miss Ferris, as if she must have the answer.

Angel waited for her response as well, wondering the same.

Miss Ferris grabbed Angel's hand with her right and Isaiah's with her left, clasping them into one clump of three. "Every one of our descendants deserves a place like Greenwood. It's up to us to make that happen."

"But how?" Angel asked eagerly.

Miss Ferris nodded toward the unfinished bike in her backyard. "There's a start. Have you finished choosing your books?"

ISAIAH

Angel chose *Up from Slavery*; *The Secret Garden*; *Peter and Wendy*; *Harriet, the Moses of Her People*; and *The Story of My Life*, and Isaiah chose *The Souls of Black Folk*; *The Talented Tenth*; *The Negro*; *The Philadelphia Negro*; and *The Wonderful Wizard of Oz*. In the end, the books made up a good balance of power and humor, Isaiah thought, a good mix for varying ages. And since he hadn't actually read *The Secret Garden* before, he'd taken it home with him that night. He'd never share this fact with Angel, but the book made him cry so hard he had to warm-iron the pages because they'd wrinkled so from his tears. He held the book to his chest and hurried out the door, heading for Miss Ferris's home.

"Going to work, Ma!" he said, attempting to leave before she called after him.

"Come here a minute," she replied. "I've made morning glories for you."

He hung his head and respectfully headed to the sweet-smelling kitchen. Isaiah had heard long ago that all mothers had a sixth sense for their evading children, but his mother was a cut above. He sat across from her at the table and folded his hands, knowing to expect questions.

"How was your first day, yesterday?" she asked, pouring herself a cup of tea. "You got in late last night."

For time to think, Isaiah stuffed a muffin in his mouth. "Just fine." He spat bits as he spoke. "You know, work."

She took a skeptical sip. "*The Secret Garden*? That's a unique choice for you. Beautiful book." She thumbed through the pages with a sweet smile.

"I really need to get to work, Ma."

"I understand," she said with much disappointment in her voice. "No time for your mother anymore. At least take another muffin for the walk."

Isaiah owed her so much more than this. Stronger than anyone he'd ever known and more patient, too, she deserved better. He settled in. "I have a few minutes to spare, actually. I've wanted your opinion on something for a while, and never quite found the time to ask."

That was a lie. He'd had the opportunity thousands of times, but was afraid that her response would be disappointing.

"Anything," she said, eager to connect. "Ask away."

"Last week, in Sunday school . . . ," he began. "You told me that I was behaving in a way that was contrary to our cause. What does that mean exactly?"

His mother looked overcome with something intensely new. Something so new that he couldn't put his finger on it. She exhaled before speaking.

"Isaiah," she said, giving herself a moment to close her eyes for a brief prayer, and a few more to admire her only son. "You have always been a fighter. Sometimes fighting battles that you shouldn't fight with young men you shouldn't associate with. I respect the fight inside of you. It's without limits, but you waste it at times."

"What do you mean, waste it?"

"Even though you know exactly what I mean, I'll try to explain." After several sips of tea, she continued. "Du Bois matches your passion. That much is absolutely true. But he's in the vein of Muggy, influencing a carelessness inside of you that has zero regard for those in your circumference. Including, sometimes, your own dear mother."

Isaiah wanted to argue. He could not. He'd heard something similar the day before around Miss Ferris's lunch table. His mother was correct about that.

She grabbed his hand. "You can be however you'd like with your ma, baby," she assured him. "As awful or as kind. But if you continue to do this with the world, you'll lose valuable allies. And if you're planning to wage war, allies are more valuable than guns."

"I understand," he said. "I've gotten rid of Muggy."

"His mother told me you two were on the outs," she replied. "She came by yesterday. Said you made quite a ruckus on her doorstep."

Isaiah seethed. "Muggy deserved every ounce of that ruckus and more, thank you very much."

"She told me that, too, in so many words."

Isaiah was shocked to hear this. "She did?"

They locked eyes. "Mothers know their sons, baby. And God made all sorts of sons—mean ones, kind ones, cruel ones, and ones that will change the world one day for the better. She's got a cruel one; that much she knows."

"Do you think you have a cruel one, too?"

"My son is a king, don't you know that? Now get to work, King, before you lose your job."

The walk was warm and thick with a dusting. No sense was left untouched in Isaiah's body. His nostrils huffed as if he were walking through a desert, his eyes puffed from the occasional allergy to Mrs. Tate's aromatic juniper, the tip of his tongue tasted earthy surroundings, and he heard whistling spirals of wind catching. The most intense of his senses, though, was in his hands.

Crossing the sandy road toward Miss Ferris's house, he kept attempting to shake the grime from his hands. They felt like sandpaper, rough and scaly. The whites of his fingernails filmed with beige dirt.

"You're late," said Miss Ferris, who'd been waiting at the front gate to let him in. "Last time, yes?"

"Yes," he replied as he walked through. "Last time."

Angel had already made it. Crouched down scrubbing at the rust on the neck of the bike, she looked less unreachable than she had for days prior. Hair free from plaits and dressed in simple blue, she was stunning, but she'd lost something he couldn't put his finger on. He was grateful, though; now, he no longer felt quite as nervous to speak to her.

"Good morning, Angel," he said. "Sorry for the tardiness."

A bit formal, he thought, but nearly normal.

She stood to greet him. "I haven't been here all that long," she said without the smile she'd worn since he'd started paying adequate attention to her.

Looking over the work she'd done on the bike, it appeared to him she had been there awhile. The thing was disassembled and almost totally free of decades of rust. "You've been busy."

"I lied," she said with her head lowered. "I couldn't sleep last night. Miss Ferris let me come by before dawn to get started. Sorry, I didn't mean to hog all the work."

"You didn't," he replied. "I should be thanking you."

"I'm going into the kitchen to make breakfast and coffee," announced Miss Ferris with an obvious wink in Isaiah's direction.

Instead of continuing to work on the bike, Angel sat on a nearby tree stump. "I needed to talk to you," she said. "Apologize, I mean. I should never have said . . . You know what I shouldn't have said."

Isaiah knew, and he was trying hard to compartmentalize it. She'd called him the worst thing she could think to call him, and it cut deep. She'd grouped him in with the enemy of their people. The worst of humanity. He could tell that she was sorry, very much so, but the comment left its mark. No one should possess such power—to burn another person with a single sentence. But she had it over him. And that terrified him.

"I accept your apology," he said, bidding to shake the comment off along with the dirt on his hands. "Let's talk about something else, please."

"Actually . . . ," she said, standing from the stoop. "I'd like to talk about Muggy Little Jr."

Isaiah had an unrelenting urge to wash his hands. Muggy Little Jr. was the worst of him. He, too, was the stuck dirt on Isaiah's hands. He didn't want to think about Muggy. Since confronting him on his own porch, he'd successfully eliminated him from his thoughts. And here she was bringing Muggy back. For the first time, anger toward Angel rose in his stomach.

"Why do you care to talk about him?" he asked, clearly cross. "He's done for where I'm concerned."

She stood firmly on both of her feet, staring at him. "We can't pretend that you and Muggy weren't insistently nasty to me for many years," she said with a calm he didn't expect. "I want to know why. Actually, I deserve to know why."

Isaiah's top teeth scraped his bottom lip in one harsh

movement. "There is no why, Angel. I can't tell you what I do not know."

He was lying, unwilling to dig into the rotten parts of himself, the hanger-on who chased bravado for acceptance. How could he be expected to expose the parts of himself he loathed? No way—not now and maybe not ever.

She took her place at the side of the bike and continued scrubbing at the fading rust. "When you're ready then," she told him.

As he watched her work, he knew something must be revealed in that moment or he would lose her. He couldn't let his guard down, but he had to be brave. Stronger than ever. She was right; after all of that hell he'd put her through, she deserved his honesty. He stooped to her side, close enough to feel the warmth of her exposed forearm. She looked at him with those eyes.

"I saw you that night." He blurted it out before he had a chance to change his mind. "Surrounded by all those boys. Did you see me?" He shook his head. "That doesn't matter, sorry. I saw *you* and I didn't help. That's what I'm trying to say. They could have hurt you. Or . . ." He softened his voice. "Or worse—"

"I didn't see you," she interrupted his rambling, and he was grateful. "I *heard* you when you opened your window." She laughed a little and playfully hit him on the arm. "The whole of Greenwood heard that window open, Isaiah. It echoed throughout the district."

He couldn't look at her. Instead, he studied the bike from

tip to tail for a distraction. Isaiah was ashamed. "I should have come down," he said. "But I hid."

Angel rested a hand on his shoulder, and that simple touch sent lightning up and down his spine. Then he thought, she shouldn't be comforting him. It should be the other way around. He, after all, had left her in the street with sixteen white boys, like a lamb to slaughter. He'd hid behind the curtain while she stood alone.

"I don't know why you'd want to be anywhere near me," he told her, avoiding her eyes. "I'm a coward. A loser. A stupid, stupid idiot."

Angel laughed again. To Isaiah, it sounded like ringing bells at Christmas. "I don't know you well enough to tell you what you are, but I think I can assure you that you are no coward. That's a dishonor few people this side of the track have to stomach."

Angel lifted to her feet and began pacing in front of him, seemingly in deep thought, carefully choosing words. "We, as Black people, carry too much guilt around with us. It's heavy, Isaiah. Generations of our fathers carried it. Our mothers and their mothers. I've noticed this, even in small children. Tiny ones like Nichelle's boy, Michael, believe it or not. And definitely you. It's an irrational and uncontrollable baggage that we cannot seem to release ourselves from."

She sat back down at Isaiah's side. This time so close he could smell her sweet honeysuckle breath. "You brought it up, just yesterday, remember? The guilt of a stocked pantry.

Even as I say it aloud now, it's a completely unreasonable thing to feel guilty about, but I get it. All Black people do." Angel covered both of Isaiah's hands with hers. "What I'm saying, or trying to say, is don't be sorry for not coming down to the street that night. You shouldn't have to hurt for hurt inflicted by sixteen boys you've never met. Let *them* have the guilt. They deserve it, not us."

Isaiah's words escaped him, and he realized he'd been holding on to his breath. He could think of nothing clever to say, so he decided just to speak freely.

"I watched you dance," he said to her, letting out a sigh. "You move like nothing and no one else matters. You're transported, shifting in and out of this world seamlessly, like a spirit. I don't know enough to say what you were born to do, but I can't imagine anyone being better at melding body and spirit and soul and song. I can't quite—" He interrupted himself. "But let me continue to try.

"My own eyes were tired from too many testimonies and entirely too much male chorus wailing that Sunday morning," he said, and she laughed loudly in agreement. "You came out of nowhere, my angel, transporting not only yourself, but me. You appeared there in the pulpit while I was kicking dimples into Mount Zion's carpet. You just, sort of, shone in never-ending white with your hair just like this."

He reached up to touch it, expecting her to swat his hands away from her head. He'd been told countless times never to touch a girl's hair, but to his surprise, she allowed it.

"Every strand floating behind you," he continued. "Fluffy like whip on a sundae."

His hand lowered from her hair to her soft cheek. He waited there, staring into her bright eyes, wondering if she would allow him to kiss her. His thumb glided to her lower lip, plump and naturally pink at the bow. He could feel her trembling under his rough palm.

"Can I kiss you?" he asked, and immediately regretted it. What a stupid thing to ask. He'd never asked a girl if he could kiss her; he just did it. Muggy would've laughed at him.

"I don't know how."

"No one knows how," he replied, shaking off thoughts of pesky Muggy. "It's a leap for all of us."

She closed her large eyes and leaned her forehead into his chest. Her scalp smelled like cocoa butter and earth. "I don't know what ready feels like, but I don't think this is it."

He briefly touched her cheek again. "You'll let me know, then?"

When she nodded, he kissed her gently on the forehead.

He then pulled the read copy of *The Secret Garden* from his pocket and handed it to her. "This book is pitiless."

She pulled back to look him in the eyes. "How could you mean, pitiless?"

"Turns the strongest men into big, ugly puddles of tears, that's how," he told her. She laughed out like a singing bird. "Not a masterpiece, but dangerously close."

"Told you."

"Yes," he said. "You did."

After breakfast, the three of them began to reassemble the bike, which turned out to be a real task for Isaiah, since his mind worked academically, not systematically. He had no idea how to contribute but refused to admit as much.

"No." He picked up a random bolt. "I think this goes here."

Miss Ferris and Angel looked at each other before easing the bolt from his hand. "Actually," said Angel, "that's the piece that holds the handlebars in place, not the wheels."

"Hey," Miss Ferris said to Isaiah. "I have an important job for you while we assemble. Why don't you take these renderings next door to Mr. Morris and ask if he'll rebuild our wooden book hauler."

He jumped up, happy for the break. "I can do that!" he said.

The dust in the air had finally settled, and he quickly reached Mr. Morris's front gate.

"Isaiah," Mr. Morris called out. "Been a minute, my boy. Come on up and show me what you've got there."

Mr. Morris's gate was in no ways ordinary. Made of hand-carved cedar and repurposed steel, it was a true work of art. Mr. Morris sat on his handmade porch swing, grinning at Isaiah's approach.

"Miss Ferris sent you with renderings, I surmise," he said, and let out a thick cough. "Well, where are they? I've been itching to get back in the shop."

Looking the old man over, Isaiah wondered if it was wise at all for him to move, let alone work with machinery.

"I can do it, boy," he told Isaiah as if reading his mind. "Been working wood my whole life."

Isaiah remained silent, not knowing the correct way to respond.

"Help me up, young man." Mr. Morris twisted his body toward the edge of the swing and held his arms in the air for Isaiah to lift him.

Both hands under Mr. Morris's hot armpits, Isaiah lifted with his legs and hoisted him to his feet. "How far is the shop?"

"Just over there," Mr. Morris said through labored breaths. "Not too far yet."

If it were only Isaiah walking, it wouldn't've taken a minute, but practically carrying Mr. Morris, it took nearly fifteen. "I need another quick break, my boy," he told Isaiah, who sat Mr. Morris down on a bench outside his shop. Isaiah needed a quick break, too.

"Phew," he said, plopping down on the bare grass.

"Here." Mr. Morris handed over the renderings. "Fan yourself with this. I don't need it anymore."

"But don't you need the blueprints to work from?"

Mr. Morris grabbed his belly as he laughed. "I said I've been doing this since I was a boy. Blueprints are for folks who don't know what they're doing. And, too, that defeats the purpose. Working wood takes a lion's share of vision. Matter fact, look at the bench I'm sitting on here." He patted his palm over the wood as if it were a living, breathing thing. "No blueprint made this. Only a God-given free mind can build beauty such as this. 'Ey now, speaking of rare beauty, I've seen you with Angel lately."

Isaiah shook his head, hoping he wouldn't express disdain toward them. Isaiah knew the town didn't think he was worthy to share company with Angel. Maybe he wasn't, but he'd hoped for an opportunity to try.

"Girl like that can turn the worst of us around," Mr. Morris said, eyeballing Isaiah in a way that made him feel uncomfortable. "*She* won't be turned around, though. You hear me?"

"Yes, sir," Isaiah replied with a bowed head.

"Well, good, then," Mr. Morris said with all of his jovialness restored. "Now that we understand one another, allow me to give you another bit of unasked-for advice. If she opens up her heart to you, hold it like you would a baby bird's. You're a young man. Not nearly old enough to appreciate such a girl, if you ask me. But if you utilize your God-given wisdom, even at this age, you'll cherish her for the whole of your life. Never let a girl like Angel go or you'll forever regret it."

"Yes, sir," Isaiah replied with as much respect in his voice as he could gather. "I understand."

Everyone in town seemed to know how Isaiah felt about Angel. Had he been holding himself differently? He looked himself over. First at his feet and legs, and then his arms and hands. He saw only himself.

Mr. Morris laughed louder in response. "My dear boy," he started. "You most certainly do not understand. You can't.

Know this, I look at you the same way you might look at a newborn babe. With a bit of pity, you see?"

Isaiah looked at Mr. Morris, confused. "I'm sorry, sir. I do not follow."

"Pity of things to come," Mr. Morris said without a hint of laughter left in his voice. "You know what they don't. You know cold, even frozen, days are not to be avoided. You know there's loss to be endured and hardship to overcome."

"Sir," Isaiah said. "There's also love."

Mr. Morris grinned genuinely at Isaiah. "Yes, there is that. But for a boy of your age, there's no angle for viewing such things as love. No hindsight in you to not take an angel for granted. We all do it, my boy; you're not stupid all alone. We all run around on the one we prayed for until she won't be run around on anymore. But you can't see that now. Live life a little longer and you will."

"I know Angel Hill is too rare to squander," Isaiah said almost into the air. "I don't even know if I'm worthy of a girl like that."

"Like I said," Mr. Morris said, shifting in his seat. "If she'll have you. Now lift me into that shed and throw those drawings in the trash."

ANGEL

ngel and Miss Ferris almost had the bike completely reassembled, and it looked brand-new.

"Would you like to screw in the final bolt?" asked Miss Ferris. "You deserve it, Angel. You worked tirelessly on this project."

"You do it," Angel told Miss Ferris. "This was all your idea."

As Miss Ferris slowly screwed in the final bolt on the left handlebar, she smiled. "I like Isaiah for you," she told Angel. "I know this is not my business. I just have to say out loud what I've been thinking for a while. You fit."

Angel thought carefully about her reply and settled on "I think so, too."

Then she thought of all of his meanness over the years.

"But do people really change that quickly, Miss Ferris?"

she asked. "He's seemingly done a drastic roundabout for my sake. I'm having a hard time believing beyond the surface."

Miss Ferris, done with the handlebar, took a seat cross-legged in the grass. "Has he shared his poetry with you?"

"Not him, actually," she replied. "Muggy took his journal from him and read one aloud. It was short, but it made me cry."

"I'm sure so," she said in response. "Even he doesn't understand their power. Isaiah has been shifting for some time, only he hasn't allowed anyone to see this. He's kept his armor on while in transition, and that's a mistake."

"I'll say."

"Hopefully, not an irreparable one."

"No one's mistakes are irreparable."

Isaiah burst through the gate with his hair covered in sawdust. He looked exhausted but happy.

"He's a genius, Mr. Morris," he announced animatedly. "Did you know?"

Both women nodded in response.

"How did I not know this?" he asked. "He showed me a few of his more intricate works, and my Lord, the man is a master with wood."

Miss Ferris stood to her feet. "You must take up time with folks to justly know who they are."

"But it doesn't take all that long to realize with Mr. Morris," Angel interjected. "He wears his virtuosity on his sleeve."

Isaiah rubbed the long neck of the now-shining bike. "This is a feat that I honestly never thought possible. Does it work?"

"Give it a go," Miss Ferris said, motioning to her flat backyard.

"Coming with?" Isaiah asked Angel.

She smiled in response. "You first. I'll watch from here, thank you."

Angel looked on as Isaiah skeptically mounted the bike. He eased himself down onto the seat slowly, not wanting to give all of his weight before testing the seat. When he finally did, the bike gave off an apprehensive creak.

"What on earth . . . ?" he asked.

"Never mind," said Miss Ferris. "Just one single lap should tell us what we need to know." She took a small pad and pencil out of her pocket. "Go on."

He placed his feet on the pedals. The first roundabout was shaky at best, but soon, it got better. Aside from squeaking and squawking, the bike rode beautifully.

"Look," he said after a few quick laps around the yard. "No hands."

Miss Ferris and Angel laughed at his childishness. Something about riding a bike could do that to a person. The wind blew his shirt tight to his chest, and he smiled with all of his teeth showing. What a lovely sight, Angel thought. And what a perfect moment in time. She closed her eyes and wished she could freeze it.

"I'd say we're done for the day," said Miss Ferris. "Get home, both of you, before you miss the streetlights again."

Isaiah dismounted and held his hand out for Angel to grab.

She thought of turning this gesture down. She stared at his hand. In Greenwood, holding hands meant something serious. It meant a relationship, exclusivity, and it meant they were going public. They wouldn't get two houses before the grapevine picked it up and spread it across town. She didn't know if she was truly ready for that or not.

She peeled her eyes away from his hanging hand and locked eyes with him. He was beaming, just like he had been while riding the bike. Tired and dirty with tiny bits of wood stuck to his shoulders, hair, and cheek, he looked more handsome than ever. Filthy yet washed clean of nastiness. If this was Isaiah, truly Isaiah, she realized she might love him. She took ahold of his patiently waiting hand and walked to the gate.

"Tomorrow and the next day, I'm helping with the Memorial Day float down at the school," Miss Ferris called after them. "See you both back here after the holiday."

"Will you be dancing this weekend?" Isaiah asked Angel before the gate closed behind them.

Angel's palm was already beginning to sweat from Isaiah's shared heat, and she could hardly focus on anything else. She'd never held hands with anyone before, not like this. In the books she'd read, holding hands was a romantic gesture reserved only for couples that wound up together in the end. But for the moment she'd been doing it, there was shared sweat and that was all.

She glanced over at Isaiah, wondering if he felt the same discomfort. He seemed so much younger than he had in the past. Like an excited child, whereas before, he'd been projecting himself older. He and Muggy did that for many years—walked with elder hunches and hanging cigars.

"What's Muggy really like?" Angel asked, suddenly needing to know more about the connection between the two. "I mean, I know he's mean as a snake to the likes of me, but what's he like when he's at his best? He can't be only unkind. No one is that."

"He's . . ." Isaiah took a moment to stare into the single cloud in the darkening sky. "I think he's in pain a lot."

"Explain."

"His own dad is . . ." Isaiah paused. "You know. Not ideal."

Angel did know; everybody knew. Angel could vividly remember a Sunday afternoon, maybe three years back, when she saw Muggy Sr. smack a young waitress on the rear with one hand while holding Mrs. Little's hand with the other. Angel remembered being mortified for Muggy's mother. She also remembered everyone around her looking embarrassed for her, too. She couldn't, however, recall Muggy Jr.'s face. And she certainly couldn't remember anyone seeming mortified for him—his father's namesake. Actually, Angel never considered that carrying a name of such a man might be hurtful. In her mind, she'd turned off Muggy Jr.'s capacity for pain. All of Greenwood had, except Isaiah.

"And he's, well, fun, I guess," Isaiah said, seemingly realizing that Angel understood the brief reference to Muggy Sr. "When he's not lost in mischief, he's actually a lot of fun."

"Explain."

"Well . . ." Isaiah started swinging Angel's hand back and forth like a seesaw. "It's hard to explain. Girls don't seem to need other girls in the way boys do. I may well be wrong about this, so don't be mad."

"Not mad," Angel replied, grateful he'd acknowledged the possibility of his wrongness. "Go on."

"I can . . ." He paused. "I could talk to Muggy about things I might have talked about with my dad. Things girls get offended by, but boys understand. Funny things. Silly things. Things I don't dare tell you about." He winked.

That was the first time he'd mentioned his dad, and Angel caught the intense, new sadness in his voice despite his attempt to gloss it over. She squeezed his hand, just now beginning to feel comfortable holding on to it. For some reason, she hadn't given the death of his father much thought. It was unlike her to overlook obvious areas of compassion, but with him, she felt off. Different in a way she couldn't understand. More flawed, less easygoing, out of character. He stripped her down in ways no one else had.

"My papa's dying," she told him, surprising even herself. "I haven't said anything to anyone, not even my mama, who helps me take care of him. It's just, I suppose, speaking about such things makes them live. Or no, that's wrong. It makes them real. More real than his diminishing stature or his graying skin."

This time, it was Isaiah's turn to squeeze Angel's hand. "I'm sorry," he said. "I didn't know."

"I'm sorry about your father, too," she said to him. "I did know."

"It's not fair to lose a father," he started, eyes glued to the ground as he walked manicured Greenwood. "I think it might be less fair to lose a mother—she's life and death. But a father can make the difference between a thriving child and a struggling one. Actually, that's another thing Muggy and I talked about. His own father works so much he's never home. He gives Muggy money and cigars and whatever he asks for, but he refuses to give of his time. And he runs around on his mother quite a lot. Muggy is very angry about this.

"My dad, though, he was everything good that a man can be," Isaiah went on, this time with his eyes toward the sky. "Treated my ma like the queen she is. He wouldn't let her lift a thing. Even skillets when she cooked. He'd jump up from the dining table and help her even when she didn't need help. She deserves that still."

Angel could tell Isaiah's mood had changed when his hand went limp. "Hey," she said, trying to sound in high spirits. "We have two blocks left to talk about something happy. Tell me, what do you plan to do after graduation? What do you dream of doing?"

169

Isaiah irately let go of her hand, surprising her. Following his gaze, she observed why he'd done it. Muggy Little Jr. and Dorothy Mae were sitting on old Mrs. Mable's front stoop, awaiting their approach.

ISAIAH

Well-worn habits crept into Isaiah, threatening to overtake him. For a fleeting moment, instinct told him to deny Angel. Pretend she'd accidentally grabbed ahold of his hand in error or desperation. He felt a familiar mischievous smile sneak across his face, forcing itself on like a too-tight costume. Then he looked over at Angel. She'd noticed his hesitation somehow. Felt his shifted energy, and that snapped him back to reality.

"May I?" he asked, again reaching for her hand.

She glanced from him to Muggy, who was nearly doubled over with laughter. Then she locked eyes with Dorothy Mae, who wasn't laughing at all. Actually, she looked about to cry. But Isaiah was grateful when Angel agreed to take his hand. So grateful, in fact, he pulled her hand to his lips and gently kissed it.

Muggy halted laughing and began clapping slowly and quite dramatically. "Well," he said. "Isn't that just sweet."

"Move along, Muggy," Isaiah said with an overpuffed chest. "You don't want to do this."

"Do what, exactly?" he replied, chuckling like a child. "Disturb your romantic stroll home with your *dancer*?"

"Leave them alone, Muggy," Dorothy Mae said in a voice smaller than her actual one. "They're just walking."

"What are you, blind?" he snapped at Dorothy Mae, who lowered her head in response. "This is no walk. This"—Muggy stuck an unlit cigar between his bared teeth—"is love. Black Angel love."

Isaiah, who was now standing right in front of Muggy, eased Angel slightly behind his body for her protection. Surely Muggy wouldn't hit a girl. He'd never actually seen that side of him, but from the looks of Dorothy Mae, something was amiss.

"Step aside, Muggy, I'm not playing with you."

"No," he replied firmly. "You step aside."

"Gladly," Isaiah said, happy to guide Angel around Muggy and Dorothy Mae, who now were blocking the path. But Muggy stepped closer to him. "I'm warning you. Don't do this."

A protective fury Isaiah only ever felt in the presence of his mother rose inside of him. Angel's hand squeezed his slightly, a warning, he thought. Or maybe fear, he couldn't quite tell without looking at her, but he didn't dare break eye contact with Muggy. To look away would be a show of weakness. Then Angel squeezed again, harder, so he looked away. And when he did, so did Muggy.

In the commotion, Dorothy Mae had snuck to the nearest house—Mrs. Tate's. The woman emerged from her juniper, curious and annoyed.

"Angel, gal," she said, her voice thick with disapproval, as she smoothed down her signature housedress and adjusted her bonnet. "What in God's name are you doing with this lot? And you, Dorothy Mae Bullock. You gaining a dirty reputation all up and down these streets. Get on home now, girls, both of you."

"Yes, ma'am," Angel and Dorothy Mae said in shamed unison as they headed in opposite directions to their respective homes.

"And you two," Mrs. Tate said, turning her full judgment on Isaiah and Muggy. "Running the streets like wandering willows, oughta be ashamed. My Timothy was never such a rascal as the two of you, thank the good Lord for that."

Muggy burst into laughter and then covered his mouth, his shoulders still bouncing.

"And just what is so funny, young man?"

Isaiah knew why he laughed. "Don't you dare, Muggy," he said. "You keep your filthy mouth shut and go home to your mama."

When Muggy looked into Isaiah's eyes, he knew he should've kept his mouth closed. Now that he protested,

Muggy would surely tell Mrs. Tate the truth about her beloved son.

"I'll go, ma'am," Muggy said. "But before I leave, I'll say this . . ."

Isaiah knew him well enough to know that he was about to inflict pain upon Mrs. Tate. Isaiah should've punched him square in the face right then and there, but just like in the curtains the day he saw Angel confronted by the white boys, he froze as Muggy continued. "Your sweet, perfect boy is just as into whores as I am."

"Lies!" she spat like a stepped-on rattlesnake. "Dirty lies from the pit of hell."

Muggy replaced his cigar and spoke through it. "You should ask your husband."

"Stop, man," Isaiah pleaded, noticing a small crowd growing. This time reaching out to touch his shoulder. "This isn't your business."

Muggy's hands shot into the air. "You're right. You're right." He smiled. "I'll just talk to him myself next time I see your perfect Timothy rolling in the brothels."

The next thing he knew, Isaiah's balled fist hurled toward Muggy's unsuspecting nose, meeting it with such force that Muggy's feet flew from under him and his head hit the ground. Senses heightened, Isaiah heard multiple screen doors squeak open and slam shut.

"What in God's name is happening out here?" someone yelled.

Another voice hollered in the near darkness, "Who's that on the ground?"

"It's the butcher's boy," a woman's voice replied. "Isaiah clocked him one."

"You all right, Mrs. Tate?" a closer voice asked, but Mrs. Tate didn't reply.

Isaiah couldn't make any of them out. He heard them, but all that he saw was Muggy Little Jr. splayed out on the ground, where he belonged. Then he felt a palm on the back of his neck.

"Son?"

When Isaiah turned around, he was surprised to see Mr. Morris leaning on a cane behind him, with sawdust in his eyelashes.

"How did you?" Isaiah asked him, curious how he could make it a few houses down without assistance.

"Never you mind, young man," he said. "You need to go. We'll handle this."

Mr. Morris motioned to the dozen or so men behind him. With a quick scan, Isaiah noticed many of his older neighbors including Mr. Morris's own son staring down at Muggy, who was now moaning.

"Kid had it coming," said one of them. "Go on home."

And Isaiah did.

ANGEL

Angel had heard about the commotion, but longed to hear it from Isaiah himself. Angel got up extra early to get ready for Sunday school. Actually, she'd been impatiently waiting for the sun to rise all night long. Varying accounts had made their way to Angel's ears, from Isaiah beating Muggy to a pulp, and the other way around. One rumor even involved Mrs. Tate beating both boys in the juniper. Angel wanted to find out what had happened from Isaiah's own mouth, and she hoped he'd be at Mount Zion that day. Her prayer was that they'd simply dispersed after the brief altercation and everyone had gone home. But if she knew Mrs. Tate as well as she thought she did, Angel knew better.

Piddling through her closet, Angel pulled down the light pink dress her mother had bought her some months back.

Her special-occasion dress, as she'd told her. Still stiff in plastic with hanging tags, the dress was too dressy, Angel told herself before hanging it back up and grabbing an old faithful brown one.

She heard a knock on her door. "Angel," her mama whispered. "You already up?"

"Yes, ma'am," she replied as she laid the dress on her bed. "Come in."

Her mama, concerned in the eyes, opened the door and stepped inside. "I love it when you free your hair," she said, smiling through tears.

"What's wrong, Mama?" Angel felt panic rising from her gut. "Is it Papa?"

"No, no. He's sleeping." Her mama softly sat on the edge of Angel's bed and patted the empty space next to her. "Please sit. We've been due a talk."

Angel obliged, moving the brown dress out of the way. "You're scaring me."

Her mama's hand glided to Angel's wild hair, still patterned from braids from the night before. "I'd always dreamed of a crown of hair like this. Soft, fluffy, and uninhibited." Then her mama's hand returned to her lap. "I don't know what I've done in my life to deserve such a girl as you."

Angel watched as her mama's gaze went to the floor. To Angel, she looked ashamed, embarrassed about something, and she'd never seen her like this. She was usually quite the spitfire, direct but somehow still charming. Never this.

"Last night I had the most beautiful dream. I dreamed that you danced with such freedom. Without a care in the world, you danced. And that was the whole of the dream. My beautiful girl dancing free." She paused. "I've allowed you to miss the best parts of being a girl. Playfulness, abandon, and, mostly, love. I let time slip and didn't think about it at all. But you, more than anyone else I know, deserve to be loved fiercely and without limits. I'm sorry I didn't see."

"Mama," Angel said cautiously. "I don't know what you mean."

"You're sixteen and beautiful," she continued. "You shouldn't have to take care of me and your father and the neighbor's screaming baby."

"But, Mama," Angel said, just grasping what her mother meant, "I was put on this earth to—"

"Help people," she finished for Angel. "I know."

"Well, then you know I don't mind one bit."

"Mrs. Tate came by late last night," her mother said. "She's a mealymouthed woman, that much you know. After declaring war on Muggy Little Jr., she told me about you and Isaiah holding hands. The rest of her rant went away, and all I could think of was you. I was angry at the thought of losing your help." A tear fell from her eye and crept down her cheek. "Without you, there's no way to stay afloat. And I'm a selfish woman for thinking this."

Angel watched her mama hide her face behind her hands. She began rubbing her back for comfort.

"It's okay, Mama," Angel said. "I think everyone thinks this of me."

"Yes." She lifted her shoulders. "But that's not fair to you. If you want to be with friends after school, you should be able to. If you'd like to hold hands with a boy that lives down the street, you should be able to do that, too. Not wasting away here with me. And I'm sorry for allowing it. From now on, no more baby Michael."

"But—"

"But nothing," she interrupted. "No more cleaning Papa with me, either."

"You can't lift him alone . . ."

"Listen to me." Her mama smiled. "You have one year left at Booker T. High School. That's all. After that, you'll be an adult. If you so choose, you may then save the world one colicky baby at a time. But this year, you get to hold hands with a boy. That's it. You understand me?"

Angel nodded.

"Good girl," she told her before getting up and opening the door to leave Angel's room. "Now get ready for Sunday school."

Staring down at the now-wrinkled brown dress, Angel decided to wear the pink one instead.

The church filled even earlier than usual that morning, Greenwood folks congregating in from the parking lot, to the church foyer, and even spilling into the fellowship hall. Clumps chattered, some holding their palms to their lips in surprise while others whispered details into curious ears.

Muggy, Angel thought. That rascal had really done it this time. That morning, her mother had implied she'd heard what actually happened at Mrs. Tate's, and she seemed so upset that Angel didn't want to ask her to elaborate. She knew, however, that it had to be bad. She then noticed a hush over the crowd as she approached. They were discussing her.

Angel had never been on the receiving end of church gossip before. It was a strange feeling, to know that neighbors, church members, and friends were creating narratives with her as the star. She quickened her steps to get to the pastor's study, where the other members of her praise dance team were congregated.

"Wooo," said Truly, the youngest. "You look like a lady!"

Betty, the second youngest, took Angel's hand and twirled her around to make her dress poof out. "So, so, so pretty!"

"Thank you," Angel told them with a smile. "Do either of you know what everybody's talking about out there?"

"You don't?" asked Truly. "My mama said you were there, kissing and hugged up on that cute Isaiah."

"That's not all they're saying!" added Betty. "They say Muggy Little Jr. got his tail beat by your *boy*friend. My daddy said Isaiah laid him out, right there on the dusty ground. My uncle helped carry him home."

Angel lost control of her legs and slid down the wall into a heap. "My God, he didn't."

"He most certainly did!" said Truly. "Mama said the boy's had it coming for some time."

Organ sounds broke into their conversation, and Truly and Betty got up to leave. "You coming?" Truly asked.

"I think I'll stay back for a few minutes."

"Save you a seat!"

They skipped into the main fellowship hall. Angel curled her knees tight to her chest, trying to make herself as small as possible. Looking down at her delicate pink dress, she desperately regretted wearing it. The brown would've blended better, made less of a splash in the already-buzzing church. She'd really picked the wrong day to fix herself up. As the congregation sang "The Lord Is My Light and My Salvation," she couldn't make her body move when the door opened behind her.

"Hey," whispered Isaiah. Angel first saw his bandaged hand and immediately knew the rumors were true.

"How did you know where to . . . ?"

"Truly," he said, smiling. "As soon as I came in."

"You're at Sunday school," Angel said, briefly forgetting all the madness happening at Mount Zion.

He placed his hands on her upper arms and said, "After seeing you dance, I'll never miss Sunday school again."

Angel watched his keen eyes watching her, but she didn't feel uneasy at all anymore. It felt right actually, him looking at her. She thought of her mother's words from that morning.

Angel had always thought it was her job to help people. Be Christlike and serve. She'd never thought of wasted time or opportunity or what she herself deserved. Looking from Isaiah's wanting eyes, to his beautifully spread nose, and, finally, to his full lips, she only wanted to kiss him, even if she didn't know how. So she did. Right there in the pastor's study even if it might have been a horrible sin.

His bandaged hand made its way to her lower back and wispy tingles traveled with it everywhere it went. His hand was streaming the best magic. His other hand rested on her cheek, and it, too, carried its own enchantments. But most mysterious of all were his lips. Soft and plump like nothing else she'd ever touched. She tried to compare them to something, but she wasn't able to. His lips moved in ways that made her never want to stop kissing him. She shifted her body closer into his, as close as possible. After a moment, he pulled away, leaving her stuck in time with her eyes closed and lips puckered.

"We should go out there before they all come looking," he whispered, blowing his sweet breath into her cheek. "They all saw me come back here. Angel?"

"Yes?"

"Open your eyes."

Angel fluttered them first and then opened to see his broadly smiling face. "Would you feel more comfortable leaving separately?"

"No," she said, grasping his hand without hesitation. "We leave like this."

"They'll talk."

She planted a quick but passionate kiss on him. "Let them."

ISAIAH

Isaiah snuck up behind his mother, who had been cleaning dishes, and kissed her on the right cheek.

"What was that for?" she asked, turning to face him.

"I love you, Ma," he told her. "And I appreciate you."

"I love you, too, baby," she said, wiping her hands and eyes on her apron. "Thank you for saying it out loud. A ma needs to hear that from time to time."

"I know," he replied. "From now on, I'm going to be helping you out a whole lot more around here. With cooking, cleaning, yard work, all of it. You keep this house a home by yourself. No way you should have to do it alone."

Instead of replying, she hugged him tightly.

"All right, now," he said through her squeezing. "I have to get to Miss Ferris's for work."

She quickly turned back to the dishes, avoiding eye contact. "Go, get on, now."

Walking through his own front door, he decided, right then and there, that he would be entirely different. No longer selfish or lazy or unworthy.

For the first time in years, he took in his surroundings. Tree-lined, kept Greenwood. His world, insulated from the cruel one Du Bois had talked about. One thing Booker Washington was right about was Greenwood. He'd called it the Negro Wall Street of America. A mecca. A beacon of hope for his people and Isaiah was blessed enough to live there every day of his life.

Passing well-loved houses filled with well-loved families, he again wondered, why him? Why did he, a seventeen-year-old rascal, get to live in such a place? At least for the time being, he decided it didn't matter why. What was important now was that he truly appreciated this rare opportunity. He would take his freedom of knowledge and spread it like wildfire to the rest of his people. Set their minds ablaze in the same way his was born free.

He'd come up on Mrs. Tate's corner lot. He smelled the juniper before he saw her sitting alone on her porch. Everything in him wanted to pretend he hadn't seen her sitting there all by herself. A few short weeks ago, he absolutely would have done. He pushed in her gate and took a seat to her left.

"How you holding up?" he asked her. Though he knew

she'd seen him, she hadn't yet acknowledged that he was there. "Didn't see you at Mount Zion yesterday."

"He had no right," she told him through clenched teeth. "No right to so easily crush a life with his words. None at all."

Muggy didn't have the right. That much was obvious, but to Isaiah, it wasn't as simple as Mrs. Tate's family revelations and new sulk. It was a lifetime of this. Ruining people's dreams and self-esteem. Twisting daggers into his own Greenwood neighbors. And for years, Isaiah was an accomplice.

"I had no right, either," Isaiah said to her. "Bearing witness . . . no. I've been equally guilty as Muggy of terrorizing my own people. With you, that was the first time I didn't go along with it. I should've punched him long ago."

Mrs. Tate shifted toward Isaiah, showing interest in his presence for the first time since he sat next to her. "You're a drop in the bucket, young man. Younger than you know. Young enough to learn how to think for yourself. Stand up against what you don't believe is right. Fight, punch, protest, whatever you want to be is ahead of you completely. Begin now and you'll make for a damn dynamic man. Maybe as good as my Timothy."

"Thank you for saying that," he replied. "I know even putting me in near the same ballpark of the same category of your Timothy is a high compliment."

She laughed at that. "Sure is. And I should be thanking you."

"Why's that?"

"Watching that horrible boy moan on the dirt brought a bit of joy back into my body."

"He had it coming," Isaiah said before getting up from the front stoop.

"He did."

Again, Isaiah was late to Miss Ferris's house, but this time she wasn't angry. As she fawned over the freshly finished bicycle, she was happier than he'd ever seen her. Next to her stood his glowing angel in a green dress that reached her ankles. As he approached, Angel waved, and he felt himself beam back at her.

"Can you believe it?" asked Miss Ferris. "Mr. Morris installed it early this morning. It's so much better than my drawing. Look at this."

Isaiah had to peel his eyes from Angel to get a good look at the wooden carrier at the back of the bicycle. It really was a wonder. Smooth at the edges with dark and light brown swirls still adorning the shiny wood. Individual, removable book compartments soldered into each rectangular stall. One was marked from birth to five, then six to ten, then eleven to fourteen, and, finally, fifteen and up.

"Mr. Morris did an amazing job with Blue," Angel said slowly and sweetly.

He could feel her eyes searching him. "He really did," he said, meeting her gaze with his own.

Miss Ferris took the moment in, grinning and clearly pleased with their connection. "Well, what are you waiting for then?" she said to them. "Load her up and deliver these books. You're both on the clock."

ANGEL

Angel had a feeling about that day. Not a good feeling or a bad feeling; she knew, somehow, that the winds of change were pending.

She'd been kissed, for one. And two, she'd initiated a kiss herself. That feeling had to be love, she thought, and since she'd never actually been in love before, she didn't know that it came with an uneasiness. Everyone under such a spell must be ill at ease, she thought. Was that why so many people acted so strangely?

"You're either thinking of something wonderful or horrible," Isaiah said to Angel as they rode Blue slowly down the dusty road. "And I'm afraid to ask."

She didn't quite know how to reply, so she placed her hand over his hand, which was holding the handlebars, and spoke about something else. "For the last few nights, I've been reading the Du Bois works you chose."

"And?"

"There's no denying his genius," she said, trying not to offend. "His words are as intellectually sound as any I've ever read. Quite philosophical."

"You don't have to say that."

"I know that I don't." Angel waited for Isaiah to bring up Booker T. Washington in response, but she was glad he didn't. It would have been forced. And she wanted only truth from this Isaiah. "It's fair since you told me about how much *The Secret Garden* made you cry." She clasped his lean arm.

"Did I say cry?" He laughed, hiding his face with his free arm. "Okay, I did, but in my defense, that book is—what's the word?—melancholy."

"Melancholy?"

"You know, gloomy. Depressing."

"It most certainly is not gloomy!" She playfully threw his arm away from her. "It's a magnum opus, as our Latin teacher would say. A work of art. Think of it: a family of wealth. A girl given anything she's ever asked for. Surrounded by pomp, circumstance, jewels, riches, but all she truly longs for is the love of her dead parents. It's a tragedy, and with tragedy comes a fair dose of gloom."

"So you agree!" he shouted. "It is gloomy."

She lightly thumped him on the upper arm and grabbed ahold of it again. "You do love to win an argument."

"It's a character trait," he said. "No use trying to fight it."

"I like it. It's simultaneously annoying and endearing."

They rolled through half of Greenwood in order to reach the less affluent blocks within the community. Angel rarely ventured into them. Typically, she had no reason to, but today she was ready to deliver books.

The dwellings in those last couple blocks of Greenwood were more shacks than houses. The yards much less flowery, most of them dusty dirt, same as the road. The people were the same as the people in her neighborhood, though. Dirtier, yes, but the same.

Kids chased one another through multiple houses' yards, playing tag while their mothers hollered after them to slow down. Lines of clothing caught air, swaying and puffing up to dry. And even though Angel and Isaiah recognized only a few of the people, they all waved and welcomed them.

"Stop up there." Angel pointed to a congregation of seven young girls sitting in a tight circle near the end of the Frisco tracks. They looked to be playing patty-cake.

Isaiah pulled close to the girls. "Hi, young ladies."

The eldest looked to be around eleven, but they swooned in his presence. He, in response, had no idea what to do or where to look, so Angel took the lead.

"I'm Angel," she started. "And this is Isaiah."

"Hiiii, Isaiahhhh," they all chuckled in unison, sending him into a full shiny-cheeked panic. He waved quickly and ducked behind the books.

"We're here to bring you the best books in the world." Angel crouched down next to them, right there in the dirt. "Hand-chosen by myself and the one and only Isaiahhhhh."

Angel caught eyes with him before he rolled his at her.

"May I sit?"

"You'll dirty your pretty dress," said one of the youngest girls in the circle. "Our dirt's hard to get out."

Angel could see the worry on this child's face. It reminded her of her own. "A little dirt in the dress is well worth the privilege of sitting in such a circle."

They all smiled up at her as if she were royalty. "I'm Sally Ann," the girl told her. "Pleased to meet you."

Then the rest of the girls took their turns telling their names—Mattie Hayes, Anna Grace, Wilhelmenia, Cora Faye, Fannie, and Hattie.

"Pleased to meet the lot of you," Angel said, careful to make eye contact with each girl.

"You go to Washington High School?" asked Cora Faye with wonder in her eyes. "That's where I'm going."

"You wish," said Wilhelmenia. "None of us going to the big school. We've got our own schoolhouse, right over there."

She pointed to a sooty shack right off the lines of the railroad track. Angel followed her finger to make sure she was looking at the right place. This was no place to adequately learn physics and history and Latin. The train whistles alone would make the environment unproductive to learning. She must've shown her disdain on her face, because Isaiah, out of nowhere, jumped into the conversation.

"We'll bring Washington High School to you, then," he said with extra exuberance in his voice. "How's that sound?"

Still swooning, they nodded in approval.

After three hours sitting cross-legged in the tight circle of seven girls, Angel and Isaiah had only covered the first few pages of *The Secret Garden*. They could barely get through a paragraph without the girls asking the meaning of a new word or even deeper questions about wealth and privilege.

Around her, Angel felt brilliant Blackness, the same as she felt in Greenwood's booming business district. From Isaiah to the other girls, all longing for knowledge, know-how, strength of mind and spirit. Books were an avenue, but not the only one. Angel wanted to introduce them to everything she loved about her own Greenwood, a couple dozen blocks away. The cushion of thick grass, the peace of planted seeds emerging slowly. This was her mission now. To reach these girls. But not only these: all Black girls, like Sojourner Truth did.

As Isaiah carefully discussed his interpretation of the book with the girls, Angel felt a tear quickly fall from her right eye. And then, through a blur, she saw ominous clouds suddenly form overhead. Teasing clouds with no condensation in them. These were the ones her papa had told her about. With these clouds came sirens.

ISAIAH

Isaiah's mother knocked on his bedroom door. "Time to get ready for the parade."

He'd been reading one of Angel's other selections, *Harriet, the Moses of Her People*. Only halfway through, he knew there was no way he'd finish it. Reluctantly, he placed the book under his pillow alongside Du Bois—a high compliment.

"I'm up. Here I come."

Everything in Greenwood had closed down for Memorial Day. All shops' blinds were lowered and shades drawn, but the streets were filled with excited people, ready for the festivities. Most Greenwood folks called it the greatest parade of the year, with baton twirlers, high steppers, and the best band in the land, from Isaiah's own Booker T. Washington High School.

The band was popular for good reason. Preparation was extensive and lengthy. The vibrations of barrel drums shook Greenwood for six weeks leading up to Memorial Day. High steppers got tongue-lashings from the band director, Mr. Monty, for being mere centimeters off their marks. Forearms were plucked for hanging lower than ninety degrees. And if twirlers dared drop their batons? Laps.

The closer to Memorial Day, the more intense the rehearsals became. The week immediately beforehand, though the final week of school, band members could be seen in steady formation before the sun rose over the school, and then in the same formations steadfast as the moon took its place.

Isaiah thought of joining the band once. He'd tinkered with flute early on in middle school, but Muggy denied him that right, calling it a girl's instrument. Thinking back, that would've been a good time to take a stand. An early adolescent rebellion could have done them both a lot of good, but alas, Isaiah simply tucked the instrument underneath his bed to collect dust. Before socking him in front of Mrs. Tate's juniper, Isaiah had thought it was impossible to stand against Muggy. But now that he had, he'd been ruminating on perfect opportunities when he could've done so earlier.

Isaiah's mother hurried ahead of him to find a rare hole in the thick crowd. Looking around, he regretted not wearing his hat since every man within his sights wore one. Though it was a weekday, the crowd wore their Sunday best. Women's waists cinched into submission, their young daughters pouting to take their bonnets off, and sons' thumbs running up and down tight suspenders.

Isaiah scanned the audience to spot someone he didn't recognize and found no one. Everyone there he knew well. But he found something new in their faces—respect. From Mrs. Edith the librarian to George Morris to the Barney sisters. His eyes rested briefly on Mrs. Tate; when his eyes met hers, she nodded and looked away toward the approaching drum majors.

Poor woman, he thought, watching her. She stood in the thick of people, forcing her chin high in the air though she knew she'd be the talk of the town for a few more days. But not for the same reason he was. She was being gossiped about while he was revered.

Donning her everyday housedress, she stuck out in the parade crowd like a gardener in the midst of church folks. She'd probably been snipping juniper all day, while reminiscing about fond memories of her beloved son and esteemed husband. How horrifying it must have been to find out it had all been a farce. She was a woman undone within moments by a loose-lipped dud named Muggy Little Jr. He deserved his ass whupping, truly.

Isaiah rarely pitied anyone, but there he was pitying poor old Mrs. Tate. That was Angel's influence, he realized and smiled to himself. The reverberating impact of a genuinely good human in one's life. The drum majors took his attention as they turned a corner and came into view.

When Isaiah was small, he accompanied his mother into the all-white side of Tulsa for a trip to the chamber of commerce. That day, for a reason he could not recall, they'd closed the streets off for a parade of their own. Isaiah remembered lots of green hats and streamers catching wind. He also recalled loud hollers and belligerent shrieks from near-drunken men fumbling all over themselves. Isaiah hid behind his mother's long skirt, still peeking with one eye to catch the sight of the white drum majors.

"Mommy, mommy." He asked her, tugging at her tucked collared shirt, "What are they doing?"

She leaned down with such grace. "They're drum majors, baby. Just like the ones from Booker T. Washington at the Memorial Day parade last year."

After thinking of this for a moment, he'd replied, "They're nothing like that, Mommy. Not at all."

She smiled and stood straight-backed.

In that moment, Isaiah remembered being sad for the white people in the green crowd. No one should have to watch such a dull sight of drum majors waving lazy hands back and forth and back and forth for no reason at all. A drum major was meant to entertain—dance, high step, and kick so high he could bloody his own nose. This was not right, Isaiah recalled thinking. Not right at all.

But now, watching his classmates Thomas Odom and Reginald Tip at work, Isaiah knew this was world-class drum majoring. For the first time since the band's inception,

Thomas and Reginald had added synchronized back flips to Washington High's already-incredible routines. Everyone's eyes widened at their unrivaled talent, including Isaiah's, even though he'd witnessed that very sequence many times.

"Never gets old, does it?" His ma elbowed him gently. "Look! How do those girls get their batons to fly so high? I always wanted to do that. No rhythm, though," she said with a small, off-tempo shimmy at the end.

"Yes, Ma." Isaiah smiled and shielded his eyes from her attempt at dancing. "I know."

"Hey!"

When the dance line came into view, Isaiah could've sworn he saw the team captain, Faye Tifton, shoot him a sly wink, and then the only freshman on the team, Lillian Finn, shoot him another. Surely he'd been imagining things.

"Is it me?" his ma whispered into his ear. "Or are these girls winking right at you one after the other? Good Lord, I guess smacking the town bully is just the love potion you needed." She playfully rubbed the top of his head, and Isaiah grinned before leaning away.

He hadn't realized how much taller he was now than her. She never had to reach upward for his head until now. Something about that made Isaiah sad.

"Best drum line in the land," she said without looking away from them.

Isaiah nodded as they marched in step with one another while beating drums and pulsating through the town. After his failed attempt at the flute, Isaiah expressed interest in the drum line. They were girl magnets—significantly more loved than any athlete at the school. But after his father took him to one lesson, he quit.

"Those guys make it look easy," he said back to her, remembering that one lesson. "Feet, hands, arms, shoulders all isolated to their own beats. It shouldn't be possible."

"Guess I'm not the only one in this family with no rhythm," she teased.

"Hey!" he replied. "You got me."

The remainder of the parade was a pretty typical small-town display—kindergarten kids waving from the sidelines and throwing candy, handmade floats rolling down the street, and people of all ages waving handheld American flags on Popsicle sticks.

The soldiers brought up the rear.

Isaiah hated the sight of them with their faded haircuts, sullen faces, and stiff uniforms, but he couldn't leave without saluting. Feet together, unbending hand to forehead, and chin up just like his father had taught him. Don't you dare cry, he told himself, as one by one they saluted back to him. Then the crowd caught on, and everyone else saluted, too. From the youngest child to the eldest adult, of one accord, everyone showed reverence to those who fought and to the memory of those who died.

Don't you dare cry, he told himself, watching his teary mother as she saluted. Don't you dare cry, he told himself, imagining his handsome father grinning with pride for his son, actively becoming a leader and no longer a follower. Don't you dare cry, he told himself as he caught a familiar smell of honeysuckle floating closely in the crowded air—Angel. His gaze followed the scent to indeed find her standing a couple short inches to his right. She, too, was saluting the fighters.

Then, still in active salute, he began to cry without apology. Soon after, large raindrops fell around the parade-goers, dispersing the crowd and hiding Isaiah's tears.

Still, he, Angel, and his ma stood there getting drenched in the sudden downpour. They watched the soldiers, most of them in their twenties, marching along as if it weren't raining at all. They'd surely been through worse, Isaiah thought.

But then the founder of Greenwood's head newspaper, *Tulsa Star*, ran toward them, yelling something indiscernible into their formation. Immediately, they dispersed.

"Wonder what he told them," said Isaiah, finally allowing his stiff hand to fall.

"Couldn't make it out over all this," his ma said. "Let's get out of this mess."

And they ran into the soda shop to dry off.

That afternoon, Angel and Isaiah had been aimlessly walking the streets of Greenwood since the festivities ended and the rain let up. Taking in the beauty of the day, they'd snaked every street, not caring one bit about neighbors or gossiping schoolmates.

Angel couldn't imagine a more perfect day. Hot, yes, but no ominous clouds teasing any more rain or pesky winds kicking up dirt. It was as if the Lord himself commanded the earth to be still so that they may have an afternoon of joy.

"That was lovely what you did, starting the salute," Angel told Isaiah, his shoulder slightly brushing hers as they walked. "I'm sure they all appreciated it."

Isaiah, however, remained silent, and Angel thought he was likely thinking of his own father. Angel had noticed that Isaiah rarely mentioned him. A tender spot, and she knew better than to bring him up herself. But she didn't have to.

"They went to the big war right along with all those white boys," Isaiah started. He'd lost the lightness, and his voice was now heavy with anger and hatred. "Probably pushed them right to the front of the lines to die. And then some came back. Expecting salutation, and instead, getting spat on like they hadn't fought for those foul folks' freedom. Used as space holders for their warm bodies and then discarded like trash. Wearing the same uniforms, carrying the same guns, and, worst of all, killing for this country. Probably killed folks who looked at them more like humans than the people they were fighting for do." Isaiah paused to kick a baseball-sized rock clear across the street and into someone's front yard. "Maybe my father was better off not seeing all of that. Better off not knowing he killed the opposition of his enemies here at home. Could you know what I mean?"

Isaiah looked at Angel with pleading eyes. Exasperated and out of breath, as if he'd just articulated something he'd been mulling for a very long time. Angel, however, had no idea how to respond. The truth was that her mind knew what he'd meant, but her heart could hardly reconcile the hatred from which it came. He seemed to view all white people as the evil enemy, put on this earth to battle and ultimately be defeated. Her perspective was different. She saw the bad ones as ignorant. Not quite victims of circumstance; that would be much too much undeserved grace, but damned by upbringing. Living luxurious lives on this side and destined to pay a heavy price on the other. Nothing to envy there according to Angel.

"I know what you mean," replied Angel. That was all she could think to say in response to such a raw reveal. She felt both uncomfortable and honored that he'd trust her with such a moment. It felt like a turning point in their budding relationship.

"My papa is d-d-d . . ." She stopped herself. It was much harder to say the second time. "Dying." She finally forced the word through her uncooperative lips. "Doctors say there's not a bit of hope. Papa says he's ready. I'm not near ready."

Angel stared at the dusty ground. Isaiah didn't say anything for a long time, and Angel wondered if he was offended that she'd changed the subject. But his father was gone and hers was going. This was the second time she'd hijacked his heartbreak and replaced it with her own.

"I'm sorry," she said, realizing her error. "I shouldn't have nicked the conversation and made it all about me."

Isaiah remained quiet, which made Angel nervous. So nervous, in fact, that she had no choice but to speak more.

"I don't know what comes over me sometimes; I just can't stop myself from talking and talking and talking. I think it's a strange tick to fill silences."

When she locked eyes with him, he smiled. "I love you, Angel Hill. I know it's crazy to say that, but I don't care anymore. I've loved you since I saw you dance. Maybe before then without fully realizing. I think I've loved you my whole life and fought it back like a weed. Scared, too cowardly to stand up to Muggy, but my heart knew when I did not. And when I saw you dance, it popped wide open. The realization of that love was a freeing thing, a relief. I think that's why I stood up to Muggy after all these years. I'm whole with you. I don't need Muggy or my place in Greenwood society. I have you. And you, Angel Hill, are more than enough."

Right there in the middle of the street, Angel Hill kissed Isaiah Wilson. With confidence and abandon, she kissed him like she knew what she was doing, which she didn't. But it didn't matter.

While kissing him, there was only the two of them. Standing in the middle of idyllic Greenwood, surrounded by beauty and Blackness and excellence and kindness and gossip and loved ones and loss and hope for the future. They were produced by the dream of this place. The unlikely optimism of the enslaved. Brought over by force, funneled through country like cattle, paid for like resources. And then, dear God, there they were.

Two intelligent, passionate Black folk. Kissing freely in the middle of the street their own people owned. What a wonderful world it was.

GREENWOOD

From your blood, I rose. Brick by brick, I was built with tired hands that deserved rest. You. Black. Beautiful. Never broken. I prayed for you to thrive and watched with pride when you did. I wanted to touch your shoulder and whisper my pride into your ear but I could not.

So, I showed myself in the quiet ways.

In the finest, most fragrant verbena, I surfaced—bright, hybrid, and with the posture of a dancer. In the tallest, most enviable juniper, I watched you smile as you breathed me in. In the weepiest soapberry trees, I hid nests of songs and spirits. And through them, I sang my encouragements—*push on, you're nearly there, push on.* I steadied the winds, giving you time to erect your paradise. I polished the soil beneath your feet so that you walked on the best I had to offer.

But yesterday.

Yesterday, a white woman's scream swung the atmosphere so far that I could not catch it. Her scream lit an already angry brew, fueling and feeding a starving mob whose hunger was not for food. Her scream echoed through newspapers, and living rooms, and up and down sidewalks until today—the thirty-first day of May in the hopeful year of 1921—when the brew has overflowed.

ISAIAH

Exhausted, Isaiah hadn't had a full night's sleep in days. Desperate to connect with Angel on another level, he'd been lost in her literature. Reading her recommended books, one after the other, and beginning to understand the crux of her argument against Du Bois.

To his delight, her argument wasn't a weak one. Actually, it held a similar strength to his. The main difference was compassion. Action, yes. Movement, yes. But also acknowledgment of an ever-present undercurrent of pain from decades of servitude. And that was certainly a palatable philosophy for Isaiah to digest.

He sat on the floor underneath his bedroom window thinking of Booker T. Washington. His hero's nemesis and subsequently his own. Isaiah perceived him as brown-nosing the white people while keeping his own within the confines of bondage for the sake of himself. A man refusing to simply forget his own circumstance and fight without restraint.

But through Angel's eyes, Washington was pushing against the pain of his youth. A pain that Isaiah had only read about in books and never actually experienced. A pain that existed in millions within his community in Greenwood and well beyond. Such pain must be adequately addressed and acknowledged, was Angel's point. And her point, he thought, may just be a valid one.

Thinking of her, his mind drifted to their kisses. He chuckled a bit at the untidiness of it. Angel had no idea what she was doing, but she threw herself into it. At first, they smashed teeth together so awkwardly that it hurt. Quickly after that, she caught her stride, and it became the kiss of his life. She tasted like honeysuckle straight off the vine, and her lips were like the first bite of freshly baked homemade bread. He could've kissed her all day long.

He felt an itch in his right hand and realized he hadn't written in a while. Opening his journal to a rare blank page, he blinked away bleariness. He'd taken in too many words over the past few nights, and his eyes were tired. Still, ignoring sleep, he set pencil to paper and began with the word . . .

Kiss . . .

A dry gust of wind came through his cracked window and brought with it the smell of evergreen burning. He placed his journal to his side and slid his feet into waiting slippers. As he stood, he bent backward to give his lower back a good crack. He needed rest. He peeked through his nearly closed curtain expecting to see a sleepy, dark Greenwood.

At first he thought the sight was his imagination. The orange glow pulsing throughout his usually peaceful neighborhood. Smoke dancing against the fiery backdrop, twirling like an angry angel defected. Faraway screams that he couldn't believe he hadn't heard before that moment. They surely should've risen him from his reading, but no, it was the distinct smell of Mrs. Tate's juniper burning that stung his nostrils awake to the chaos. He'd never taken in such a horrible scent or sight. Amazing, Isaiah thought, that the juniper that had won prizes for its beauty and color could produce such an ugly fragrance when destroyed. He imagined that scent would never leave. It would somehow stay forever, floating in the wind from house to house like the fire was now.

In the far-off distance, he squinted to see a line of what looked like bouncing lit matchsticks. After much confusion, he understood that they were men holding torches.

"My God." He whispered something close to a prayer over Greenwood. "My God," he said a second time before running to wake his ma.

ANGEL

Angel couldn't sleep at all after that kiss, so she stayed up reading *The Souls of Black Folk* to better understand Isaiah.

On the surface, he came off militant and unruly. But earlier that afternoon, he'd broken himself down, sharing the most challenging pieces of himself with her. He loved her and she believed.

Through clanking teeth and sloppy lips, she regretted only one thing—not telling him she loved him back, which she did. I love you, I love you, I love you! Such an easy thing to say, so why on earth hadn't she said it?

On her way home from the kiss, seven of her neighbors stopped her and asked about Isaiah. To her surprise, their comments were lovely.

Mrs. Turner had told her, "That Isaiah sure did stand up for Mrs. Tate, huh?"

And then Mr. Morris said, "He helped me to my wood-shed. Nice boy now that he shook loose that Muggy."

Even Deacon Yancey kept it kind by saying, "Still don't like him, but he showed a flash of character at that parade today."

Angel grinned, thinking of the town she loved. The town where everybody knew everybody's business and she didn't mind one bit.

As she looked up from the book, lost in her thoughts, her bedroom began to glimmer a strange amber color. New light caught the corners of her dresser and the foot of her bed. The lights were bobbing like apples on water. Up and down and down and up, dipping in and out of view.

She lifted herself from bed and peeked through the crack in her curtains. She found herself staring into a bright blue eye. A wide-eyed man pressed his face on the outside of her bedroom window, holding a handmade torch in one hand and a large baton in the other.

Angel screamed without trying to and ran to her mama and papa.

ISAIAH

Isaiah never entered his mother's room without knocking, but that night, he did. When he opened the door, he saw her lying atop the covers, curled in fetal position. A slight smile lifted her face in her dim room.

Isaiah wanted nothing more than to let her sleep. He wanted to shut the door behind him and allow his sweet ma to bring her last pleasant dream to a close. He didn't want her to know what he now knew—beloved Greenwood was burning. The only space for Black Tulsans in the white imagination had become too successful. Too much of a threat, so now it, too, was being taken away, just as his father had predicted.

In the distance, he heard a wailing and knew he should wake her. But instead, he quietly closed the door and then glanced at his watch.

"Two minutes," he whispered into darkness. He would give her two more minutes to smile in her sleep.

In the front room closet, Isaiah found his father's extra-large military duffel bag hanging on the inside hook. He wasted a moment to breathe it in. It smelled like strange oil and sweat. The fabric of it was soft like it had been dragged around many places, and it was empty except for his father's clanking dog tags.

Almost instinctively, Isaiah bowed his head and put them on, as if knighting himself. He wanted to fight. For his smiling, sleeping mother. For his benevolent, bright angel. And for his sweltering Greenwood.

Moving quickly around his house, he began collecting necessities—dried beans, rice, and six loaves of fresh-baked bread. Then he turned his attention to the memories over the fireplace.

Photographs of himself as a baby, then a toddler, then a child, and then now. Fragile newspaper clippings of his saluting father's obituary and funeral program. His father's medals carefully lined along the mantel like hand-tall soldiers. Isaiah rarely allowed himself to look there. It was too hard to remember, but now that he was forced to, he realized there was nothing representing his ma. Not even a photograph with her in it. He glanced at his watch to see that his two minutes were nearly up. He needed to find something sentimental for her sake. Something representing the quiet power of her love. The bag of food and memories simply was not complete without that.

Isaiah took one last look at his small, quaint home. "Thank you," he whispered in the darkness. He wished he could grab it all and stuff it in the bag. The wool knit throw with blocks of bright colors folded on the arm of the couch. The side table he hit his head on when he was learning to walk. He still had the scar to prove it. This, he knew, was probably the last time he'd see it all. "Thanks for everything," he told his sweet home.

Gently opening her bedroom door, he found her still smiling in her sleep. He glanced over her to see a wedding collage framed at her bedside table. Within it was his mother and father's singular wedding-day picture, a swatch of lace from her dress, and the handkerchief from his suit. Peeking from the borders were their vows, handwritten on thick, expensive paper.

Isaiah lifted it into his bag, then squatted at her side.

"Ma," he whispered, wanting to wake her with as much calm as possible. "Sweet, sweet Ma."

She stirred and grinned, still dreaming what seemed to be the sweetest dream. He placed a gentle hand onto the top of her scarfed head. "Ma," he said a bit louder. "My love, you need to wake."

Her eyes slowly snuck a quick look through long lashes and closed again. Then she burst awake as if realizing the strangeness of his presence at her side. "My God," she said in panic. "What's happened? What's the matter? Are you hurt?"

"Not me," he said as calmly as possible. "Greenwood."

She shook the remainder of her sleep away and asked, "What could you mean, Isaiah? How is Greenwood hurt?"

Instead of answering, he rose to his feet and opened her white curtains to reveal their scorching community. At first, her eyes squinted in confusion but then widened with knowing.

"We need to go," he told her. "Now."

"Where?" she asked him as if he were the parent and their roles were reversed. "If not Greenwood, where do we flee to?"

It was a good question. As Isaiah stood there holding the heavy duffel bag, his thoughts jumbled into themselves for the first time since he'd smelled the scorched juniper. Where could they go? How would they coordinate with everyone else? How would they know they weren't running toward the enemy?

His hands began to cramp from being clasped into such tight fists. His knee buckled a bit, weak from the weight of his father's absence. He shifted his gaze to the twirling flames in the distance and attempted to place them.

The flickers burned brightest to his east. From the smell of the juniper, they'd gotten to that early in the night, which meant they should avoid Mrs. Tate's house at all costs. Then he realized Mr. Morris's woodshed would serve as exceptional kindling for the flames, and the old man would surely need help getting out. And they were just down the road from Vice Principal and Mrs. Anniston and their newborn. Isaiah briefly closed his eyes and said a small prayer for their new family.

And then it hit him. "My God," he said to his ma. "Angel."

In response, she stood and looked out the window. The flames shone brightest near her street. "It could be too late."

Isaiah ignored the comment, even though he absolutely had heard it. "Get dressed quickly. I'll go get cloth to cover our noses from smoke." He hurried toward the hallway pantry. "I'll be waiting by the front door. And, Ma . . ." He paused, staring into her shocked, twinkling eyes. "I love you."

He hurried to his duties before she had a chance to say it back.

ANGEL

The sinister blue eye staring into Angel's private bedroom terrified her into near hysterics. Heart pounding, she cried out and ran to awaken her parents. Making her way down the hall, she picked up the sight of converging torches surrounding her small home. The house should be dark, she thought, but instead, it was a radiant orange and as hot as a skillet.

She burst into her parents' bedroom, startling them awake. As soon as their eyes opened, they began to understand. The smell of burning buildings overwhelmed Angel's nostrils, and the orange was as bright as the first flash of sunrise. The worst of all, however, was the chorus of screams.

Those screams belonged to her church members, her classmates, her teachers, her doctors. They belonged to the people who made up the beautiful and complicated periphery of her lovely life. The loudest one, though, came from the mouth of her mama when she saw the blue-eyed, torch-wielding man standing directly behind her only daughter. He'd made it into the house.

Angel turned to see a scrawny man hardly taller than herself. Without the torch and steel bar, he would surely be unthreatening, Angel thought. A paper tiger with no power to speak of if it wasn't for his race. Angel hated this man without knowing him.

He grabbed her forearm and threw her to the floor toward her parents. "Time to go."

That was all he told them. *Time to go.* That was all they got from the trespasser in their home in the wee hours of the morning. Angel stood back up tall, facing him with as much strength as she could muster.

"Where are you taking us?" she asked, fighting to keep her voice from shaking.

"None of your goddamn business is where," he replied, the heavy stench of liquor filling the room. "Now get up 'fore I burn it down with you three in it!"

Angel's mama stood to the left side of her ailing husband. "Angel," she said with surprising calm. "We will have to lift him."

Dutifully, Angel crouched underneath her father's right shoulder and together she and her mother lifted his limp body from the bed.

"Please," he managed to say. "Leave me. Please."

The intruder stood in their doorway, grinning with snuff-black teeth. "He's right, you know? Ain't no use trying to move him. We're burning this whole damn place down. You two need to run if you got a chance in hell of surviving this night. And can't run holding dead weight."

"Leave me," her father said, staring deep into her eyes. "Your mother won't. You have to."

Angel's mother looked at her. "Don't you dare do it, Angel. We can all make it out of here together. You hear me?"

Both of her parents were pleading with her. Both asking the unthinkable. One, to leave her precious father and let him burn. And the other, to defy him because he couldn't put up an adequate fight otherwise.

"I can't hold him myself," her mother said, crying intensely. "I need you or I'll drop him. Please, Angel, please."

Then Angel looked at her father. He was smiling at her. His was a smile that could light up a dull room and bring joy back when there was none to speak of. The same smile she'd seen on every Sunday afternoon when her mother set his heaping plate of food in front of him. The exact same one Angel had seen when she sat for hours listening to his philosophies and wisdoms. The smile that gave her hope when the whole world seemed to think she was too strange to exist.

She leaned in to kiss his grinning cheek with as much tenderness as she could find inside of herself, and she did as he told her to do. She released him, giving the whole of his weight to her mother, who buckled underneath it.

Angel hid her face behind her hands, attempting to veil her pain from witness of the white man in her doorway, but her chest betrayed her, bobbing from crying as she watched her parents' embrace. There was no air between them, and Angel could hear them whispering *I love you*s back and forth into one another's necks.

"We don't have all day," announced the man in the doorway. "I've given you more than enough time to say goodbye. Now get!"

As Angel's mother released her father, to her surprise, he stood on his own. With both feet firmly planted, he took two impossible steps forward, accompanying his wife and daughter safely past the intruder. Angel's mother walked ahead, crying hysterically, and disappeared out the front door.

"I love you more than life," her father said to Angel, who had just made it to the living room. "Watch those sneaky gray clouds for clues." He winked to his daughter and then turned his gaze to the prowler who was just a few feet away from him.

Angel watched as her father grabbed the intruder's torch and lowered it to his face, burning the white man's mouth into a screaming blur.

"Angel! Go!" her father yelled after them. "Run!"

She ran into the yard, found her mother, grabbed her shaking hand, and ran toward darkness, away from all of the orange.

ISAIAH

"Mount Zion!" Isaiah announced as his now-dressed mother reached the front door. "I think that's where everyone will go. And surely they won't burn down the Lord's house. They call themselves Christians, after all."

Down deep, Isaiah knew his words were empty and false. He'd read enough to know that the hypocrisy of such evil provided no cover even for sanctuaries of worship. Still, he needed to provide some comfort to his mother. True leaders projected confidence, even in the most hopeless of places. Mount Zion was the best his own frazzled brain could come up with.

He placed his hands on her shoulders. "Ready?" he asked.

She nodded without words, and they exited their spotless home for what they knew would be the last time. Crossing the yard, Isaiah looked up at the leggy tree outside of his bedroom. For a fleeting second, he prayed for God to spare that tree for its beauty and memories.

When he was small, he'd used the enormous rocks at the base of it as lifts to reach the lowest-hanging branch. When his calloused palms caught good grip of it, he swung his legs atop, and from there, climbing was easy. He remembered the first time he built courage enough to stand, hands free, on the highest branch. *You'll break your neck*, his father had said, never actually telling him to get down. He saw pride in his father's smiling eyes. He saw that his father was honored to have a son so brave.

"Please, God," Isaiah whispered to the burning wind. "At least save the tree."

The feel of the night was strange since the darkness had been forcibly stolen by bright flames. Isaiah and his mother felt eerie calm as they ran down the center of the street. Aside from a few figures in the distance, his side of Greenwood still slept. The reflex to stop at crosswalks crept into Isaiah's gut. The pull to raise his hand to wave at neighbors, and maybe pick a stem of verbena for his ma was strong. Such instincts were ingrained into him, coursing through his veins as a part of his being. He wondered if he'd ever be able to shed them fully. Then, memories came.

Passing elderly Mrs. Edward's mailbox, the light from the not-so-distant flames illuminated the permanent scorch left after he and Muggy had blown it up. It had been Muggy's idea—Muggy brought the supplies, Muggy devised the plan, but it was Isaiah who'd lit the final match. He thought of poor Mrs. Edward, cozy under one of her handmade blankets, waking the moment she was about to burn.

To his left was Dorothy Mae's house, the only two-level tower on their street. Dorothy Mae's parents valued opulence, and the grange house told the tale with its pointed shrubs and crisp shutters. Isaiah thought of Dorothy Mae stealing from him, upending his life as he knew it. He thought of her as sinister, sneaky, and crafty, using her beauty and soft lips as keys to locked kingdoms. But then he remembered. She wanted to fly. How she got up there didn't matter, she'd said. A product of Greenwood, she, like Isaiah, was desperate to be set free.

Next door to Dorothy Mae was the small, eclipsed home of Bloody Mary. A few down from her was Annie Carlson, the bad poet from his English class. Directly across from her was Scott Hall, who he'd cruelly locked in the filthy bathroom stall back in middle school.

Isaiah let go of his ma's hand and stood frozen in the midst. "You need to go ahead," he told her.

"What?" she asked, stunned. "No!"

"These people have no idea what's coming," he said, nervously fiddling with his father's hanging dog tags. "I need to at least wake them so they can have a chance."

His ma nodded at her late husband's tags, recognizing there was no use trying to stop her son. She knew him better than anyone else on earth did. And she knew when he'd made up his stubborn mind.

"I'll help you," she said.

"No," he objected, handing her the loaded duffel bag. "You need to get to Mount Zion and gather more supplies from the kitchen and stockroom." She stepped forward to interject. "More than that." He reached his hand to her soft cheek. "You need to tell everyone I send to you what's what. They will be frazzled and confused when they get to you. Maybe even still in their nightclothes and slippers. You have to help them be ready for many difficult days as I know only you can."

She looked him over, first skeptically, and then respectfully. "Where did you come from, my sweet, sweet boy? You shouldn't have to be a man yet."

"You shouldn't have had to be both for so long," he replied. "Now go! I need to wake these people up before they die in their beds."

ANGEL

"HOW could you?" Angel's mama kept yelling as neighbors ran away from their smoke-filled homes with only the clothes on their backs. "Angel! We could have all made it out."

Her mama was in a full mania, absolutely unable to be consoled with words or touch or anything else Angel could think of. Angel then turned her attention to the approaching men with torches. They'd already made it past Mrs. Tate's home. She couldn't see the house from there, but she could smell the juniper burning stiff on the air.

"We have to go, now," Angel told her mama before grasping hard on her upper arm. In response, she violently twirled herself onto the grass and into a weeping, unmovable bulge.

A mix of people were running in the streets. Neighbors she knew from as far back as she could remember. Loved ones who sat in the same pew at church jogged past her and her mama, searching out which direction to go. Then there were white men in the crowd as well, menacing. In direct comparison to her neighbors, who looked completely caught off guard, to Angel the intruders looked prepared for the chaos. They approached an strategic clumps of three, and others hung back for an alternating ambush.

That's when Angel entered a strange headspace, somewhere between daze and shock. Her mind went blank, and there was no hope left within her. She couldn't tell how much time had passed, but the smells strengthened. Swirling within the burning juniper was now the smell of cooking meat. Human flesh, she realized. Or maybe unfortunate pets caught in the charred massacre. Intense, panicked thoughts began to swirl in her head.

She had just killed her father.

She'd released him to crumple. Against the will of her precious mother, who now hated her. Of course she did. Angel had allowed the singular love of her life to burn in her childhood home. She may as well burn with the rest of it.

Then, piercing the veil, were familiar screams. Baby Michael! It was as if someone had stuck Angel in the side with the tip of a brooch pin. She spun to search for him. Mrs. Nichelle stood stunned on her front porch, holding wailing Michael like he was her only piece of treasure left in the world.

Angel squatted to her weepy mama's side. "I have to check

on Michael. Cry now, but when I get back to you, we're leaving this place together. You hear me?"

Her mama didn't respond. Angel hurried to Mrs. Nichelle.

"Where's Mr. Anniston?" Angel asked, out of breath.

"I-i-inside . . . collecting supplies."

"There's no time," Angel told her. "Michael's yells are making you all a target. You need to go."

Mrs. Nichelle stared into Angel's eyes like she hadn't slept in months. "What's happening, Angel? Why are they doing this to us?"

Angel knew she had no time but couldn't resist the urge to comfort her. "The why is of no importance here," Angel said, forcing a smile and placing a gentle palm over Michael's sweaty forehead. "All that matters is that you get your little man to safety. That's your only job, Mrs. Nichelle. The burning doesn't matter. Not even Greenwood matters. You just survive to raise this little boy into a man so he can build a better Greenwood one day." Michael halted his sobbing and calmed as if accepting the charge. Angel glanced around to see men, only three houses down, lighting shrubs ablaze. "You have to go."

"My Lord," said Mr. Anniston, just appearing on the porch, holding an overstuffed pack. "Where will we go?"

"Mount Zion," said Angel, knowing well from her readings that nowhere would be safe, not even the Lord's house. "We'll meet up there." She looked around at the destruction. "Those of us who make it, I mean."

Just then, her mama's voice rang through the chaos. "Angel," she said, not quite shrieking but not in a normal tone, either. "How can I . . . ? What should I . . . ?"

"No time for apologies," Angel told her pleading mother. "You need to get to the church. Mr. Anniston, will you ensure my mother makes it there safely?"

"You have my word."

Angel locked eyes with her and said, "I love you, Mama. See you very soon."

"I love you, too, baby."

Before her mother could fully gain her bearings, Angel headed in the opposite direction, away from Mount Zion.

"Where are you going?" her mother yelled after her. But Angel kept going without answering.

In the distance, she heard her mother again ask the same question. And then a third time. Her mother could have done it a fourth, too, but Angel was out of earshot. She needed to go. She needed to help.

ISAIAH

Isaiah banged on elderly Mrs. Edward's front door and, after a few short minutes, circled the small house to bang on windows instead. Easily pushing seventy, Mrs. Edward was hard of hearing, he remembered.

"Mrs. Edward!" he screamed, bashing the glass.

Like a chorus, the neighboring houses' lights flipped on from his yelling. He was killing multiple birds with one stone. Encouraged, he began to holler even louder. "Mrs. Edward! Wake up!"

From surrounding houses, Isaiah heard the repeating chorus of *What's that racket?*, followed closely by knowing sighs of astonishment toward the approaching flames. He didn't have to tell them a thing. Within seconds, they smelled and saw the destruction for themselves. Isaiah's job was to startle as many residents awake as he could so they could see for themselves. But Mrs. Edward wasn't responding, and he wouldn't dare leave her to burn.

Though she never knew he'd lit the fuse to blow up her mailbox, he'd wronged her. She was always kind and quiet, never bothering another soul with gossip or worry. Mrs. Edward deserved better than to spend money she didn't have on a new mailbox and lawn. She deserved better than to burn herself. And Isaiah owed her. The day after he'd done it, Isaiah waved and smiled at Mrs. Edward like he hadn't ruined one of her possessions. Back then, he'd felt a mixture of shame for doing it and cleverness for getting away with it. But now he was desperate to save her.

Numerous households were awakened by his screams, but Mrs. Edward's home stayed dark and quiet. *Wake up,* he thought in his frantic mind. *Wake up so that I may make amends. So that I may be freed from your debt.*

ANGEL

Angel watched from a far distance as Mr. and Mrs. Anniston took her mama and baby Michael in the direction of Mount Zion. The inferno around her had spiraled into utter confusion and terror. Lavalike, liquid heat dripped from dead streetlamps while shadowy figures, some holding children and elderly parents, scattered without instruction. Windows burst from the pressure of the flames, turning loving homes into what looked like fiery demons spitting their inhabitants into the streets. Within hours, her exquisite neighborhood had taken on the heat of hatred and been transformed into hell.

"Lord help" was the best she could do for prayer, and then she ran.

Her night slip was drenched in sweat and clung to her

body. Even in the scramble of loss and impending death, she was horrifyingly aware of her near nudity. Surely the good Lord would grant her forgiveness under the circumstances. He'd put her on this earth to help, and if this wasn't her opportunity to do just that, she couldn't say what was.

As she ran, she passed gone houses with families standing lost in what used to be their yards.

"Mount Zion!" she screamed whenever she caught sight of another paralyzed group holding on to one another. "We're all meeting at the Mount!"

The dark, thick smoke left behind by torches choked her dust-filled lungs as she ran. She needed water, but still, she never stopped running and yelling the best destination she could think of, hoping it was the right one.

Hyperaware of her surroundings, she kept catching the enemy in her periphery. Peeking through bushes, congregating between burning houses, and some even walking down railroad tracks without care, grinning and pointing at the destruction they'd caused. How could they burn such a place? she thought between coughs. Du Bois was right. Isaiah was right. And her beloved Booker T. Washington was more wrong than she ever could've imagined.

There was no way to live peacefully alongside the foe. No building by one's own bootstraps or rising from ashes. Washington had been guessing, just as she was about Mount Zion. Leading Black folks toward something he didn't truly know existed, and watching the fire seep through every crack of

Negro Wall Street, she instantly recognized he'd guessed wrong.

"Mount Zion!" she hollered over her anger, seeing another tightly grouped clump of terrified neighbors. "Go to the Mount! Mount Zion!" she said, spotting the shadow of a little girl, all alone in her yard. Squinting, she tried to make out the obscure figure of her, shaded and outlined with angry orange as her backdrop. A quick flicker of light passed the young girl's cheek. "Truly?"

Angel jogged toward her with arms wide. The closer Angel got to Truly, the more she saw her, heavy with pain. She didn't want to ask, because she could read the answer on Truly's face. But Angel had no choice at all.

"Where are your parents?"

Truly didn't answer immediately. Instead, she hung her tiny head and sobbed like no child should have to. "Daddy went back in to help Mommy."

Angel crouched to her knees, eye level with seven-year-old Truly. "How long ago?"

"Too long," Truly replied.

Angel briefly toyed with the thought of trying to save them. She saw her papa, standing again before scorching that intruder's mouth shut for good. She felt a selfish gratitude for having her mama and papa for sixteen whole years, while this poor child, in the span of a few minutes, was likely orphaned. Angel leaped to her feet and began running the circumference of Truly's house, searching for any sign of life left inside.

Nearly the entire home was engulfed; the only entry point was a raised window in a tiny back bedroom. Peering inside, Angel saw a figure and blinked. Surely there could be no way.

"Mrs. Arnold?" Angel yelled into the black smoke. She had to be dead in the midst of such swirling smolder. "Mrs. Arnold!"

No response to her voice. The sounds of wood creaking above teased a cave-in of the roof, but still, Angel stepped out of her slip and wrapped it around her face, and climbed into Mrs. Arnold's bedroom.

ISAIAH

S treaks of blood were left behind with every new knock on Mrs. Edward's door, but Isaiah wouldn't abandon her. He owed her, and if he let her burn, he would owe her for as long as he had left to live. In the distance, Isaiah heard a confused crowd growing.

"Lord have mercy, tell me I'm dreaming this."

"How could they do it?"

"Not here," someone repeated over and over. "Not here. Not here. Not here."

Isaiah wanted to turn around and tell them all to shut up their complaining. Of course here. If not Greenwood, where? It's textbook. Stamp out the most prosperous among us, and the rest lose hope. Eliminate the talented tenth, and there you had it, eternal servitude. Did these people not read Du Bois?

A gentle hand startled him. Hyperalert, he'd assumed it was the white folks and swung at the eerie figure.

"Calm," the familiar voice said to Isaiah, who still hadn't placed it. "It's just me."

Muggy, he realized. Isaiah hadn't thought once of Muggy at all in the midst of this.

"This is no time for games, Muggy," Isaiah said through shaking teeth, his continuous knocks leaving small clumps of skin behind on Mrs. Edward's door. "Go away."

Muggy grabbed Isaiah's wrists and held them in the air from behind. "Her hearing, Isaiah. She's nearly deaf."

Isaiah snatched his wrists out of Muggy's grasp. "So leave her behind, huh? Run for your life while this poor woman burns with the rest of them. But who cares, right? She's just an elderly, hard-of-hearing old fool, isn't that it, Muggy Little Jr.? Well, you go. You run! I'm staying here. I owe this woman."

Muggy lifted a large, crisply sharpened butcher ax from the leather bag crossed over his shoulder. "I owe her, too, Isaiah."

Muggy drew the terrifying weapon back and brought it down hard and fast onto Mrs. Edward's wooden front door, breaking it open.

ANGEL

Angel grabbed ahold of Mrs. Arnold's limp feet and began to drag her toward the wide-open window. To Angel's surprise, she wasn't heavy. Her weight in the chaos seemed lighter than baby Michael's, and lurching her dangling legs over the sill and out of the frame seemed easier than it should have.

She heard Mrs. Arnold fall onto the porch in a heap, and then she heard the creaks of faltering wood above her. Her body easily slipped through the window after Mrs. Arnold, and Angel grasped her underneath her armpits and began to scream for help, expecting no one to come.

The whole of Greenwood was consumed with their own infernos. Angel kept dragging her until she reached the middle of the backyard. Her tired, dry lips met Mrs. Arnold's, and she began to blow as much fresh air into her lungs as she could breathe in. Then she pounded her chest with flat palms, praying she was doing this correctly.

As she pumped, she thought of Truly, alone in the front yard. Truly's little life flashed before her. There would be struggle. More than any child should ever have to endure. She would have to navigate this horrible world with only her tiny hands and not-yet-developed female body. A perfect target, she was. Without protection from men, she would be ravaged, and soon. Angel began to cry tears onto Mrs. Arnold's still cheeks. This was Truly's mother lying on the ground before her. The child's singular hope for a life worth living.

"Mrs. Arnold," Angel said as she pumped her chest as hard as she could. "I need you to come back from wherever you've gone. No time to dawdle; you've got a baby girl standing alone. A girl is never an easy thing to be, Mrs. Arnold, you know that. Especially a Black one. You, ma'am, need to walk away from the gates and come back here to raise up your Truly. If you don't, she will be spit out."

Again, Angel breathed in new air and leaned over to share breath. She blew until her lungs emptied and she felt a rising in Mrs. Arnold's chest. Then she repeated this, as many times as God told her to. There was nothing and no one else in the world at that moment. Just Angel and Mrs. Arnold, Truly's last hope. The thought of giving up never crossed into her mind. Not once. She would breathe for this woman until this woman breathed for herself.

And all of a sudden, like a spark catching fire on a rock, Mrs. Arnold's body came alive, shooting up and gasping for its own air. Angel yelled out incoherently, and someone appeared by Mrs. Arnold's side to help.

In the slight light, Angel recognized Miss Ferris's green glasses. She'd brought a large glass of water and held it to Mrs. Arnold's dry lips. A few other neighbors surrounded Mrs. Arnold, and Angel nearly fainted from giving away most of her own oxygen.

She fell away from them into a heap and stared at Mr. and Mrs. Arnold's home giving way to the fire. It went down with a dramatic crash, as if deciding to go out with a bang. The sparks made Angel squint, but she didn't close her eyes to it. Her eyes were wide open.

While she was catching small sips of burning air, someone covered her body with a large, white fitted sheet. Somewhere in the bedlam, she'd lost the slip she'd wrapped around her mouth. It was likely burning with the rest of the Arnolds's home. But thank the Lord, Mrs. Arnold was coughing and alive. She couldn't see her, but she could hear the loud rattle of her lungs breaking phlegm free to clear her airways.

Still heaped on the ground, Angel caught sight of Truly running through the back gate and screaming for her mother. She ran like she was running toward hope and away from sorrow.

The crowd parted for her, and she met her mother with a promise never to let her go.

Angel—put on this earth to help people—rose from the ground, wrapped herself in the sheet, and began to run.

"Where are you going?" asked Miss Ferris, who was still crouched next to Mrs. Arnold and Truly.

"To get Blue," she yelled, coughing. "I'll use Blue to carry people. Is your home—"

"Not yet, but it will be. A heaviness came over Miss Ferris's shaded eyes. The back door's open; go in and get clothes."

"Yes, ma'am," Angel coughed out.

"And, Angel," Miss Ferris yelled after, "you're the best of us."

ISAIAH

Muggy went into Mrs. Edward's first, still holding his large butcher's ax. Together, they fanned off in different directions to find her.

"In here!" Muggy yelled out to Isaiah.

Isaiah quickly followed Muggy's voice into Mrs. Edward's sitting room, where she was very much awake, watching the flames grow. Rocking back and forth in her chair, she hummed "A Charge to Keep I Have" as if she weren't panicked at all.

"Mrs. Edward?" Isaiah approached the strange sight slowly and cautiously. "Why haven't you come out?"

She glanced around to them and smiled, pointing to her left ear. "You'll have to speak up, young man."

Isaiah crossed the room in two strides and crouched at her feet. "If you stay here, you'll die. We need to run. Now."

Mrs. Edward again smiled and placed her age-wrinkled hand over the top of his. "The arthritis has taken the whole of my body. My running days are done."

"Well," injected Muggy with a familiar air of grandness. "I'll carry you."

"You're sweet to offer," she started. "But you need to help somebody worth helping. My life has been full and lovely, you see? Contentment is my most cherished possession, and I'm just fine with dying here today."

"I won't hear of it!" yelled Muggy.

"Young man," she said, not smiling anymore. "You don't speak to your elders like that, not even in this." She motioned toward the flames. "You've got to get where I've gotten to. Walk the hard journey I have walked. I deserve your respect, do you understand me?"

"Yes, ma'am." Muggy softened, to Isaiah's surprise. "I do."

But Isaiah understood Muggy's anger. She wasn't allowing them to save her. More so, she wasn't allowing them penance for destroying something that belonged to her all those years ago. She was blocking freedom from them.

"We're the ones that burned your box," Isaiah blurted out, and then hung his head as low as it would go.

"I know that," she said. "I wondered when conscience would catch."

"How did you know?" asked Muggy.

She laughed. "You know so little, don't you? You pretend well, but at your core, you know only bluster. Young man, I sit here most days. Rocking, looking out, waiting for the Lord to walk up my front steps and take me home. I saw you when you did it."

"So why not tell anyone?" asked Isaiah, knowing he was wasting valuable time but unable to leave without knowing.

"Contentment is an earned thing," she replied. "Not something you get without accumulating years' worth of scars. The way I figure it, bombing my box and regretting it were on the path to yours." She looked wide-eyed out the window at an airplane circling in the night like a bird locking onto prey. "You two need to go. Help as many folks in this town as you can."

Isaiah stood and walked to the doorway, knowing she couldn't be convinced.

She grinned again. "Don't worry. I forgave you the moment you did it. Now get."

Muggy and Isaiah left Mrs. Edward alone in her home.

ANGEL

As promised, Miss Ferris's back door was open. As Angel crossed the threshold, she stepped out of the sheet. Again naked, she went searching for Miss Ferris's closet. Angel quickly found it and threw on the first thing she saw, a pair of gardening overalls and a long white shirt.

As she went to leave, she passed the stocked pantry and gathered an armful of canned fruits and as many loaves of bread as she could tuck underneath her chin. As Angel crossed the back door, Miss Ferris's tiny library caught her full attention. Actually, just one book within the library did— *The Secret Garden*.

She hurried to the bike, loaded it with food, and ran back inside to collect the book. Then, almost instinctively, she gripped *Up from Slavery*, *Peter and Wendy*, *The Negro*,

The Philadelphia Negro, *The Wonderful Wizard of Oz*, *The Story of My Life*, and *The Talented Tenth* from their shelves. The other two, *The Souls of Black Folk* and *Harriet Tubman*, were at Angel's and Isaiah's houses, unreachable. She couldn't bear leaving the books she and Isaiah had chosen so carefully and meticulously for their shared summer job. She couldn't image them scorched and unrecognizable. She carried them to the side basket and took the few moments to organize them in the back of the bike by category.

It was a shameful waste of time, she knew in her gut, but she didn't want those evildoers to take this from her, too. When she was done, she mounted the bike and headed toward the parts of town Miss Ferris had sent Isaiah and Angel to hand out books.

As she pedaled, she visualized those seven young girls in the patty-cake circle. All the way on the other side of Greenwood, they were likely oblivious to what was approaching. She couldn't remember all of their names, but she could see them in their beds. Stacked head to foot, burning away into unsuspecting ash. She pedaled faster, passing more destruction than she ever knew could exist.

The farther she got from her own massacred block, the quieter Greenwood became. Pedaling through a choked, dry throat, she could've been leaving the entire setting behind her. As the blocks became less affluent, the smoke cleared and heat cut.

She felt a tinge of guilt knowing she'd be the one to wake

them with such horrifying news. Slowing her pedaling, she began to feel sharp shooting pains in her thighs and forearms. Then the warmth of dripping blood wrapped her hands, and her palms slid back and forth across the handlebars. Somewhere in the commotion, she'd pierced deep, long cuts into her body. The long white shirt was pink in places and bright red in others. It crossed her mind that they might not open the door for her. She herself looked terrifying.

But there was no choice. She leaned the bike against the side of a redbrick house with dirt as grass and began banging on the front door.

"Wake up!" she yelled. "Greenwood is burning! Greenwood is burning!"

As soon as the lamplight came on inside of the home, she went on to the next house and repeated her lament. After many houses, she found herself in the same spot where she'd met the girls in the circle.

She thought of Truly's small family, caught off guard and forever fractured because of it. A new energy came over her. She would not stop until she found each of the girls. Until she witnessed their deliverance to some semblance of safety.

Louder and with more passion than before, again she yelled, "Greenwood is burning!"

ISAIAH

With Mount Zion in eyeshot, Muggy and Isaiah, along with the rest of the crowd, ran toward the refuge of the church. In silence, they fell into a familiar stride, running on the same feet like they were on Mr. Monty's drum line. Isaiah couldn't help but feel comforted by this familiarity. He didn't want to feel that way, but the sentiment seeped in all on its own.

"You socked me one," Muggy said, not angry but not amused, either. "Sucker punch if you ask me."

Isaiah couldn't apologize for punching him. He should've done it long ago, and an apology would be insincere at best.

"You deserved it, Muggy."

The Muggy that Isaiah knew would've bucked that comment to the ends of the earth. Thrown a tantrum of blamelessness and created a scene of some sort, right there in front of their newly tormented town. But in response that night, silence.

Their displaced neighbors collapsed onto the steps of the church one by one. Some holding tight to frightened children and others alone in hushed shock. Running to the cross, Isaiah thought, where the burdens of their heavy hearts rolled away. Muggy stopped at the foot of the entrance, and for all their years of friendship's sake, Isaiah stopped alongside him.

"They've burned my father's shop," Muggy said in a voice too calm for his fiery personality. "It's the only street that smells in any way normal. Like Fourth of July barbecue."

"Sorry." Isaiah meant it, but it was all he could say as he watched the crowd. The knees of the truly Godly buckling underneath the evil of lesser men.

"I came looking for you," Muggy said before reaching back into his satchel. "Found this."

He lifted Isaiah's singed journal and handed it to Isaiah with the care given a newborn. Isaiah saw himself, hurrying through his faultless home like a madman, stuffing necessities and memories into his father's duffel bag. How could he have forgotten this? he wondered. There was no rhyme or reason.

"And this, for what it's worth . . ." Muggy handed over the dusty flute that had been unblown since he'd told Isaiah it was a lame instrument.

Isaiah lifted the case from Muggy's soot-blackened hands and held it. The casing was warm and fogged along with the night. He wanted to open it, but there was no time. Instead, he tucked it safely under the front steps of the church.

"It's not a stupid instrument," Muggy admitted. "If you were going to be in band, I wanted to be in it, too. That's all. If you were going to hand out books on a bike, I wanted to do it, too. And if you were going to fall in love with a dancer, you'd leave me all alone."

Isaiah locked eyes with Muggy's. "Look around you, Muggy," said Isaiah before placing a gentle palm around the back of his neck. "I would never leave you alone. We're all we've got."

"Isaiah!" Over the turmoil, he heard his ma's voice calling out to him. "Isaiah! We need your help!"

Muggy nodded as Isaiah skipped three steps at a time to get to her. She'd transformed the sanctuary into a triage of sorts, just as Isaiah knew she would. Elderly church mothers being tended one by one in the front-most pews. Small children tucked away in the pulpit in a tight circle with the kindergarten teacher, Mrs. Merritt, in the center holding their attention. And the injured in the back being wrapped and bandaged by Dr. Owens, Mr. Tate, and his son, Timothy.

Isaiah's ma motioned him to Mrs. Turner's severely burned hand. He'd last seen her on Memorial Day, handing out free red and white flowers at her shop. Hers was the shop where his father bought his ma a single yellow long-stemmed rose every Friday for no reason at all. Sometimes the roses lasted more than two weeks and she'd be able to gather together a skinny bouquet for their kitchen counter—the dull, drying ones nestled right next to the fresh, plump, new ones.

Isaiah thought of all the flowers cut by Mrs. Turner's hands. All of the birthdays brightened, anniversaries remembered, the babies welcomed to the world with the work of them. All of the random Fridays. Now they were cooked flesh with cloth melted into their crevices.

"We don't have sedatives here," his ma told him in a rush. "We need help holding her so Dr. Owens can tend the wound."

"She bandaged it while it was still sizzling," Dr. Owens announced to Timothy. "I need a few still moments to pick the remnants before the cloth heals inside. Five minutes would do."

"Mrs. Turner," said Isaiah's ma, "bite down on this stick, please. And look away."

Isaiah grabbed ahold of her right upper arm while the other men held the other and both legs. As the doctor worked, she screamed so loudly into the thick stick that it echoed in the sanctuary. The children could no longer be distracted by Mrs. Merritt's entertainments. Their curious little eyes popped up from the height of the pulpit to investigate. Mostly everyone else's, too, with the notable exception of the cluster of elderly mothers set apart in the front.

That's when seventy-eight-year-old Mother Williams, always the first to testify on a Sunday morning, began to sing:

> "A charge to keep I have,
> A God to glorify,
> A never-dying soul to save,
> And fit it for the sky."

Never to be outdone, eighty-year-old Mother Jackson joined in, followed closely by Mother Evans.

> "To serve the present age,
> My calling to fulfill.
> O may it all my powers engage,
> To do my Master's will."

Then the entire church, some only humming loudly along, united with them.

> "Arm me with jealous care,
> As in Thy sight to live;
> And O Thy servant, Lord, prepare,
> A strict account to give."

The sanctuary sounded like a Sunday. Holding down Mrs. Turner's thrashing arms, Isaiah briefly closed his eyes and envisioned it. Sunlit maroon carpets so thick he could kick his initials into it. Testimony after testimony singsonged for everyone to know and amen. And Angel. Spinning Greenwood's thirty-five blocks into something much more confusing and complicated.

> *"Help me to watch and pray,*
> *And on Thyself rely,*
> *Assured if I my trust betray,*
> *I shall forever die."*

"Where is my Angel?" he said to himself aloud as the doctor gave the okay to release Mrs. Turner, who had nearly passed out from pain.

ANGEL

After what seemed a very long time, Angel had only found the oldest of the seven girls, Hattie.

Angel crouched to her knees to meet Hattie's gaze as her parents looked on in terror. "Can you point me in the direction of the others?"

Wrapped in a child-sized knit blanket, Hattie pointed at three houses across the street and three more to her immediate left. "They all in there," she said in a small, concerned voice.

Angel said, "Thank you, sweet girl," before standing to speak to Hattie's parents. "Only the necessities. Changes of clothes for all of you, food that will keep, and cherished photos. Nothing else, you hear?"

They nodded, staring off at the blazing distance.

"After you've got everything, meet me right here on the lawn," she told them. "If I'm not here yet, you"—she gave Hattie's father her full attention—"knock on five doors. Tell them what I've told you, and send them right back here."

He nodded without words as Angel backed away from them.

"Miss?" asked Hattie's mother. "Can I get you a cup of water? Or a fast change of clothes? You look like you've been through hell."

Again, Angel look down at her spoiled clothing. "Thank you, ma'am," she said, still backing away. "But I've got work to do."

Angel started with the house directly to their left and began to bang. Quickly, the porch light illuminated, and a curious eye peeked through the side curtain. "Greenwood is burning!" she yelled into the frightened eye, and she moved along to the second and then the third to do the same.

Crossing the street, she kept yelling, hoping to awaken more without having to knock. "Greenwood is burning! Greenwood is burning! Greenwood is burning!"

At first, her mind refused to register the weighty three words forcefully bursting through her lips. They were words of utility, not meaning. Three words strung together for the sole purpose of waking those who still slept, that's all. But as tiny lights from inside sleeping homes blinked on, one by one, she thought: Greenwood *Is* Burning.

She stopped running and stood still with her breathing.

Way off in the distance, she saw an airplane approach. Slowly circling, out of reach and range. She tilted her head as she watched it. To Angel, the airplane looked like a dirty bird circling its prey. It would be unheard of, an attack from the air. And Greenwood stood no chance against it.

A moment earlier, she'd known it couldn't get any worse. Drunken men or evil men or drunken evil men laughing as they bounced torches up and down quiet streets would be enough. The smell of burning juniper and the burning bodies of her and Truly's father would be enough. Freshly popped purple verbena shriveled back into dust would be enough. But this . . .

Focusing her eyes, she saw the thing that the airplane was circling so meticulously. In the crosshairs, the shining bell tower with the gold cross that was shined weekly. The plane's likely target—Mount Zion Baptist Church.

"Dear God, what have I done?" she said before turning Blue around and yelling to Hattie's father. "Wake as many as possible! They're about to bomb the church from the sky!"

"Ma'am!" he yelled after her. "Where should we all go?"

She didn't answer nor did she look back. She couldn't bear to see young Hattie, still holding on to her tiny baby blanket for security, so displaced. Besides, what would she tell him? Her initial thought was the Mount. She'd sent countless families there already with the fleeting hope that it may be spared. If she didn't reach them in time, she'd sentenced them all to certain death, just like she had her own father.

The menacing plane continued circling the bell tower like a lioness locked on prey. She pedaled so fast the bike screamed back at her, cautioning its age and breakability, but she ignored it. Selfishly, she now wished she'd taken Hattie's mother's offer of water. Her throat felt like she'd swallowed steel wool and sandpaper in a single gulp. Angry at herself, she pedaled even faster toward the church. Approximately seventeen blocks remained between her and Mount Zion's evacuation.

She leaned left to cut through the Avenue, which she'd been actively avoiding. Logic told her that they'd certainly target the thriving community center. That was the whole point, she'd long surmised, to steal it all. Possess that which didn't belong to them, from the drugs in Williams Drugstore, to the carvings in Mr. Morris's woodshop, for the people of Greenwood to continue to serve at their leisure.

Angel wanted to protect her heart from witnessing such inequity happening in real time, but a turn through town would shave off three blocks. As soon as she saw what was the start of booming Greenwood Avenue, tears streaked her temples. More burning, yes, there was that, but more than that was shameless looting and robbing of hard work. White men stacking crates of stolen tools from Mr. Odom's hardware shop into their automobiles. Sipping taken sodas and licking pinched ice cream from Williams. They even thieved bagged suits and hats from Mr. Massey's dry cleaner.

But the sight that made Angel most angry was also the

most unexpected—white ladies ravaging sweet Mrs. Turner's beloved flower shop. They'd walk in grinning and emerge holding beautiful bouquets of fussed-over flowers. Angel paused, wasting precious moments to watch the strange sight of white women in Deep Greenwood in the wee hours of the morning. She watched as their men cleared the way for them. Checking shops and boutiques twice over and then sending the women in to take what they wanted before it was all destroyed.

Angel knew that the women would pretend themselves blameless afterward. Hiding in their homes, knitting and rocking or whatever on earth they did across the Frisco tracks. But there they were. Right alongside, stealing the work of Greenwood's hands.

Angel honed in on one long brunette woman. She was long in everything—height, hair, even her nose was long, nearly touching her upper lip. She held a handful of purple dresses taken from Trisha's Boutique. It was as if she'd carefully shopped the racks for everything purple. And then she emerged from Mrs. Turner's flower shop holding tight to a bright purple bouquet.

What this long woman didn't care to know was Mrs. Turner would've happily given her the bouquets, free of charge. Mrs. Turner didn't care one bit if her patrons could or could not pay. More than money, she longed to inject beautiful into the forgotten places. And here they were, scrambling to steal from the most giving among them.

Then, bouquet in one hand, and dresses in the other, the too-long white woman pointed obnoxiously at the sky and began to leap up and down like an eager child. When Angel followed her finger, she saw the bottom of the airplane preparing to drop its bomb, and she pedaled on for dear life.

ISAIAH

Isaiah found Angel's mother in the back corner of Mount Zion with Vice Principal and Mrs. Anniston and baby Michael at their side. She was inconsolable, and Isaiah imagined he knew why. Like nearly blind Mrs. Edward, there was no way Angel's father could've made it out in his condition. Isaiah imagined he'd rather die than be carried out of the house by his wife and daughter, as Isaiah himself would have.

"Mrs. Hill." Isaiah approached her with caution. "I'm so sorry to—"

Vice Principal Anniston held up his hand to stop the statement and stood to take Isaiah away from her. "She's just lost her husband," he confirmed, still speaking in the same authoritative tone he used as vice principal of Washington High. "She needs time. I assume you're asking about Angel. If I'm correct about this, she's doing what any of us would expect her to do."

"What?"

"Out there somewhere." Vice Principal Anniston smiled. "Helping."

Without another word, Isaiah turned on his heels and ran toward the exit. Standing frantically on the front steps of the church, he squinted through smoke-filled air and scanned the town. His instinct was to run out into the night, searching for her, but which way could she be?

His feet carried him to the bottom steps and then halted in defiance. Wrong, his feet told him. You'll just get it wrong.

Then he saw a figure piercing the smoke in the distance. The figure wasn't walking; it was instead riding a strange contraption that looked like . . .

"Blue," he said before loping toward her.

Nothing else mattered to Isaiah, only cutting the distance between them and holding her tightly in his arms. The closer he got to her, though, the more he realized that this was no lovely reunion. This was an emergency, and it showed all over her face.

"What is it?" he asked after seeing the fear deep down in her eyes. "My God, Angel," he said to her bloodied clothing and painful-looking cuts. "You'll need stitches all over."

"The plane," she said without halting her pedaling.

Isaiah had to jog to keep up with her, and he was now

running in the direction of the church. "We've seen it. It's circling."

"You don't understand, Isaiah," she said, pleading with her eyes. "It's circling the Mount."

True terror entered Isaiah's body, and again, his feet took over, leading him back to the church at the highest possible speed. As they reached the front steps, Dorothy Mae and Muggy stood together looking horrified.

"What is going on?" asked Dorothy Mae, her hands shaking at her sides.

"Look up," he said to Dorothy Mae, remembering her longing to fly. "Angel thinks they'll drop a bomb. Is it possible?"

Dorothy Mae stopped moving and shielded her eyes for a better look at the plane's underside. "Dear God," she said simply.

"Get everyone out!" Angel yelled as she pushed past her.

Angel followed by Isaiah followed by Muggy followed by Dorothy Mae burst into the sanctuary to let everyone know that the one place they all thought they could be safe was about to be destroyed.

MUGGY

Muggy followed closely behind Isaiah, taking in all of the skeptical eyes scrutinizing his every move. Who did they think they were anyway? Looking at him like he was some sort of criminal. They had so much more to worry about than him. And they wondered why he'd hardened. They should hold a mirror to their noses, and they'd see why.

Then he looked again and began to question his own intuitions. He saw Timothy Tate consumed with wrapping burns and lesions. He saw George Morris tending his father's blistering feet. He must've been hurried from his home without shoes. Everyone busy with the hope of survival. Maybe they weren't scrutinizing him at all. Maybe, just maybe, they were looking to him for leadership, direction. He lifted his chin, ready to leave all of the hurt behind and step into that role.

"They're about to bomb the church!" Muggy announced before Isaiah had a chance to. "Everyone needs to get out."

Expecting pandemonium, he braced for the rush, but no one moved a muscle.

"Isaiah," someone said from the thick of the congregation. "What's happening?"

Isaiah shoved Muggy aside and began his own eloquent speech. "The airplane above"—he pointed to the sky—"is circling. Angel spotted its target to be most likely where we are standing now."

An audible gasp ran about the audience. The gasp Muggy himself had expected when he'd announced the same impending event just moments earlier. Isaiah would've denied the attention. Maybe he didn't even notice it, Muggy thought, but Isaiah was always favored by the people of Greenwood. They loved Isaiah while they loathed him. Daily incidents like this had been happening since they were children. Slights from the hands and mouths of those who should've believed in him.

When they were very small, Muggy mimicked Isaiah's charming head tilts and his annoying usages of *ma'am*s and *sir*s, but it didn't work. Everyone saw through Muggy. His own father told him to stop being such a follower. To think for himself. To use his head for more than a hat rack.

His father beat him with the relentlessness of a prize-fighter until he wasn't a follower anymore. And when Muggy turned mean, his father grinned and bragged about his leader of a boy. Strong, he'd called him. Now that his father had beaten the weak out.

The thought of his father made Muggy's blood boil. He'd hung on every flawed word he'd told him since childhood. Even the most outrageous dodging of rules and responsibilities. But looking around the sanctuary, he saw his mother stood alone.

His father had ducked out before the massacre altogether by disappearing with one of his mistresses the night before. Muggy and his mother knew the drill of it. Take over the butcher shop for a couple days while he took the train down to the coast alongside a woman with no name.

"Take care of your mom," he'd tell Muggy with a tip of the hat. "Be back in a few days."

But he shouldn't have to take care of his mom. That was Muggy Sr.'s job, after all. But his father benefited from the title of "married man." The delicious meals from a loyal wife. The beauty of a well-run home by a well-dressed spouse. But when the town burned, he was nowhere to be found, likely catching wind and sipping brown with she, her, whomever.

Muggy's mother stood near the organ, poised and seemingly not frazzled at all. Posture was one of the only weapons in her arsenal, shielding her from town judgment associated with a cheating husband and mischievous son.

Watching his mother standing near the choir stand, he knew she'd been punished enough. By him and by his father and by this town, surely she had. As if sensing his gaze, she lifted her hand to wave at him and held hand to chest with pride, and she mouthed something to him. There was no way to hear over the scrambling crowd, so he elbowed his way to her.

"I'm proud of you, son," she said, calm and easy in the midst of the free-for-all. "So proud. You speak like a revolutionary."

"They didn't listen to me." Muggy looked to his feet. "They hate me, all of them, and they should."

There was no room left for phony bluster or unfounded arrogance. Raw truth was all that could be spoken in times like these. Besides, she likely knew all of this. She'd always been a watchful woman. Never one to step in and fix the broken things. The type to instead wait for those around her to come to their senses and change themselves. An admirable trait if she'd married a better man. A man like Isaiah's father had been, or like Angel's, or Dorothy Mae's. Even dead they were better than his own.

"You'll have the opportunity to make it up, son," she said with such dignity. "We need to go before what happens happens."

The church had nearly cleared with the exception of the Mothers of the church waiting too patiently for someone to help them along.

"Go on ahead, Mom," Muggy told her. "I need to get these ladies out."

One by one, Muggy guided the Mothers along the aisle, through the foyer, and down the front steps.

"Stop biting your fingernails, boy," said Mother Williams as they slowly made their way along the maroon carpets. "Release hold of your worries."

Muggy hadn't realized he was doing it. It had been a habit he picked up long ago, and it showed up now only when he was terrified. He looked down at Mother Williams's wrinkled hand as she squeezed his.

"There's time for you yet," she told him. "Still yet time."

He led her to the bottom step, and Dorothy Mae took her over to the rest of the Mothers.

In that moment, he felt more connected to Greenwood than ever before. Not because he was wealthy or well-off, but because he was in the trenches with them. All of them, from the Mothers to the smallest of children. He stood watching them as they fluttered around one another. Even in the face of destruction, the ingenuity, the kinship of Greenwood folks reigned. And finally, he was a part of it.

After the last person was assisted, Muggy joined Isaiah, Angel, and Dorothy Mae, who'd congregated a few houses down from the church. They were in active debate when he showed up.

"The school will surely be next," said Angel with expressive, flailing hands. "This whole place will be gone by morning; the school's as much a target as the church."

"Don't say that," injected Dorothy Mae with much hurt in her voice. "You don't know that."

"She does," said Isaiah. "She's right, and you know she is."

"Oh!" Angel spotted Hattie's father, huffing after what seemed to be a lengthy run. "This is Hattie's father. One of the girls from the patty-cake circle," Angel told Isaiah. "Why have you come?"

"We're . . . going to the field." He panted between words. "We saw a group headed down there until they stop their burning."

Isaiah spat on the ground. "They told us to go to the field—why should we go where they say we can go?" he asked. "They don't own us. We're free! We could go clear across the world if we wanted to."

"Look around you, Isaiah," Angel told him. "Look at our mothers. Their mothers! We need to help them survive the night before we even think of revolution. There are people in the town still sleeping. Think of them first, not us."

"I passed whole streets of folks who haven't yet awakened," said Hattie's father. "There'll be lots of death by sunrise."

Muggy looked up at the circling plane and wondered why it hadn't yet dropped the bomb through its open shaft. Then he caught sight of the bronze church bell atop Mount Zion Baptist. Framed with brick and glowing orange from the reflection of flames, it called to him as the answer.

His mother had told him he'd get his chance to make it right, and the shining bell was the way. Muggy knew he himself had been burning Greenwood from the inside, long before the white men showed up with their torches. One neighbor at a time, he'd sown so much discord that there was only one way to gain penance, and looking above, the opportunity was fleeting.

"Go to the field," he told Isaiah, Angel, and Dorothy Mae. "Take everyone there and survive. That's all that should be done on this night. I have an idea for those still sleeping."

Isaiah stepped forward in protest. "Whatever you're planning, I'll help you."

"Isaiah," Muggy said, holding Isaiah's face in his palms. "You're better than me. By leaps better. You know it, I know it, Angel Hill certainly knows it," he said in her direction, smiling. "Dorothy Mae, you do, too." Their attention was briefly taken by the sound of the menacing plane above. "Let me be better," Muggy said. "For this night only, let me be better."

Grudgingly, Isaiah nodded and let him go.

Muggy scanned the crowd to find his mother and ran to her. "Mom!" he called after her. "Mom! I need to tell you something."

She narrowed her eyes, reading something within him. "What are you about to do?"

He smiled at her quiet wisdom and kissed her on both cheeks. "I love you, Mom. I really, truly do."

"I love you, too," she replied, sensing a dangerous reflex in her son. "Please don't."

She couldn't know what he was about to do, but still, she knew to tell him not to. He grabbed her into a tight hug and ran back into the church, taking the steps three at a time, all the way up to the bell tower.

ALL

ngel, Isaiah, and Dorothy Mae joined Isaiah's ma to tell her they were going to the field. Isaiah's ma had become a facilitator of sorts; everyone looked to her for instruction and direction.

"Everyone," she said over the chaos. "The only safe place left is the field. We have to walk, so if you're able-bodied, find someone who isn't and help them along. I need nods from everyone! George, you take Mr. Morris in the bike . . ." And she went on assigning specific townspeople to specific jobs.

Isaiah and Angel watched the crowd nod to her command and march toward the field. Dorothy Mae walked ahead to check in on her own family, who thankfully was still intact. Her father and mother got out unscathed with the clothes on their backs, and her younger sister had the presence of mind to grab the comforter and light blue, fuzzy doll from atop her bed. Isaiah and Angel watched as her whole family held their arms wide and embraced her upon approach.

"That's nice," Angel said, almost to herself. "Some families are still one." She looked over at Isaiah with full eyes. "That's hope."

Isaiah wrapped his left arm around her, allowing her to relax into him for support. As they briskly walked, they held one another, stealing a moment to breathe in what was left of the now-unbreathable Greenwood.

"I love you, too, by the way," she said into the nape of Isaiah's neck. "I wondered if I'd have a chance to tell you that. I love you with all of my heart, Isaiah Wilson."

With the Mothers of the church being carried, the crowd walked slower than Isaiah and Angel would've preferred. But they would not disband. This was their community now, and community stayed together regardless of circumstance.

Angel glanced back at the church, but she could only see the top of the bell tower glistening like a beacon. Then a figure inside grasped the rope and began ringing the bell louder than it'd ever been rung before. The slow-walking crowd of townsfolk all looked up to investigate the noise, and then, as if in concert, looked up to see the plane drop even lower over the church.

"Muggy," Isaiah said. "No!"

Isaiah released Angel from their embrace and tried to run back to Mount Zion, but he was stopped by Deacon Yancey.

"Let him do what he's meant to, boy," Deacon Yancey said, his voice deep with emotion. "And you do what you're meant to."

Isaiah easily pushed around the deacon, but he was then halted by Vice Principal Anniston.

"Deacon's right, son," Vice Principal Anniston said. "Let him be."

It was harder to pull himself around the vice principal, but once he did, Mr. Morris, held up by his son George, protested as well.

"You will not interrupt what that boy's doing up there," he told Isaiah with so much force he nearly fell backward. "He's made up his mind to ransom what's left of his time to save the multitude. No greater love than that."

As the bell tolled, the Mothers began to sing again.

> *"There is no greater love,*
> *There is no greater love,*
> *There is no greater love,*
> *No greater love."*

Angel then stepped alongside Mr. Morris, silently in agreement. And then, with heavy tears, Muggy's mother joined the stand.

> *"No greater love,*
> *Than a man would lay down his life for a*
> *   friend."*

As the bell continued to ring and the plane circled still closer as if warning Muggy of his impending death, the town sang on.

> "No greater love,
> No greater love,
> No greater love."

Isaiah knew they were correct, but his heart stopped still.

"We have to walk on," Isaiah's mother announced.

The townspeople did as they were told, but didn't stop singing the three words, *no greater love*, over and over again. This time, Angel wrapped her comforting arm around Isaiah and led him onward. Heavy feet led Isaiah for blocks, and he began to think the plane wasn't going to drop the bomb. Maybe, just maybe, it had all been bluster from above and Muggy would survive.

As he walked on, Isaiah realized Muggy's bell was working. Porch lights ticked on one by one as they passed what had been dark houses, and whenever a curious nose cracked open the door, someone from the crowd would yell, "Greenwood is burning! Greenwood is burning!"

And someone else would yell, "To the field! To the field!"

All broken between the chants of *no greater love*, the tolling of the bell and the humming of the plane's engine.

Muggy Little Jr. had already saved more lives than likely anyone else within the town. His idea was a brilliant one. His execution, perfect. The courage that it took to drag that heavy rope back and forth with death closing in on him, Isaiah couldn't fathom it.

The town would never recall Muggy's misdeeds now, no matter how horrible. His mischief paled in comparison to the bravery he'd exhibited this night. Mr. Morris was right to stop him, Isaiah realized. Muggy needed this moment. Deserved this moment.

With the field finally in sight, Isaiah and Angel smiled at one another. They'd made it. All of them, together, from the Mothers to the tiniest children. They filed into the field, mostly with no earthly possessions, but grateful still somehow.

But their brief beam of hope was darkened by the sound of the bomb dropping atop the Mount. The townspeople gasped in unison, and Isaiah yelled out.

Isaiah couldn't tell the difference between sunrise and Mount Zion exploding.

ANGEL

DIGNIFY AND GLORIFY COMMON LABOR. IT IS AT THE
BOTTOM OF LIFE THAT WE MUST BEGIN, NOT AT THE TOP.
—BOOKER T. WASHINGTON

Angel sat, bandaged and sewn, in the middle of a circle of giggling girls. Reading the saved copy of *The Secret Garden* to them aloud. Ages ranging between six and ten, the girls didn't find the book depressing at all, like Isaiah had. They instead reveled in the descriptions of place and person.

Every one of them hung on Angel's every word, and every few pages, one of their tiny hands would shoot into the air with advanced questions. Angel was proud to sit in that circle, discussing that which she loved and saved with them. To carry them away to better places than this. Tell them to close their eyes and imagine smells and sights and sounds of *The Secret Garden*. Then, like clockwork, one of the girls would interject . . .

"Do you love Isaiah Wilson?"

"He's cu-u-u-ute!"

"I like his eyes!"

"I like his whoooole face!"

Angel, as if dangling a juicy apple in front of them, would whisper to them, "I like his whole face, too."

"OoOooOo!!!!!!" they'd say. "Angel's in love!"

And she'd lose them for a giggling while. They were so young, Angel thought. Displaced and lost, but still whispering and chuckling about the cuteness of a boy. Angel smiled at that. Hope, she thought, in the midst of what some might see as hopelessness.

One of the girls pointed at Isaiah in the far left corner of the field.

"What's he telling them? I wonder," Truly said to the circle of girls.

"Probably how beautiful his Angel is," Hattie said, laughing. "She's all he talks about, after all."

As they went on whispering, Angel began to wonder, too. Isaiah stood postured before a group of ten men. He spoke expressively, and they looked up to him like a congregation looked to its pastor.

"He's not talking about me, girls," she said to them. "But he's saying something important, that's for sure."

She beamed in his direction.

ISAIAH

I BELIEVE IN LIBERTY FOR ALL MEN; THE SPACE TO STRETCH
THEIR ARMS AND THEIR SOULS; THE RIGHT TO BREATHE AND THE
RIGHT TO VOTE, THE FREEDOM TO CHOOSE THEIR FRIENDS,
ENJOY THE SUNSHINE AND RIDE ON THE RAILROADS, UNCURSED
BY COLOR; THINKING, DREAMING, WORKING AS THEY WILL IN A
KINGDOM OF GOD AND LOVE. *– W.E.B. DU BOIS*

"The world we live in now, gentlemen, will not be our world for long." Isaiah forced an invisible rod in his back to straighten it before ten men much older than him. "We've seen what life is supposed to be for men and women and children and families. For humans. We've tasted glory. Peace. Held them both precious in our slippery hands, and we will grab hold of them again, men, heed my words.

"Every family represented here is a light of knowing," he said with as much might as he could build from his gut. "This, my friends, is more important by leagues than any brick and mortar. This, men, cannot be burned away from us. You see? It was not our homes or our businesses that the white men were trying to steal away that fateful night. No, it was the knowing they saw building up within our bodies. The posture elevating our shoulders back to neutral. Back, friends, to where they'd been before they pushed us on boats and brought us here.

"Booker T. Washington once said that 'one man cannot hold another man down in the ditch without remaining down in the ditch with him.' This is dead to rights but unfinished. What Washington left unsaid is, sooner or later, the focus of the held-down man eventually shifts. Through battle, his arms lean and develop muscles strong enough to propel him out, leaving his captor there alone to rot in his rage."

"But shouldn't we go back?" Deacon Yancey raised his hand to ask Isaiah as if he were in school. "Now that we have no place, should we return to the land of our ancestors?"

Isaiah observed the men nodding to the deacon's suggestion. He took it in for a moment, and smiled knowingly. "My dear deacon," Isaiah started, "this is our land now. We would be foreigners in the lands of our ancestors. Without language or knowledge of customs, we'd be starting over. Unwelcomed, sadly, by those we were taken away from all those generations ago."

The same men that nodded to the deacon's idea, now shifted in agreement with Isaiah. "That's a valid point you have there, young man," Deacon Yancey said, again sitting quietly.

"They brought us here"—Isaiah stood over them like a father among sons—"to build a country from nothing.

To work the lands, shepherd the sheep, and, dear God, to breed. They did not, however, anticipate us." Isaiah held his arms out wide and spun around, highlighting now-scorched Greenwood.

The other men looked around to see only ashes in the distance. No buildings left standing or homes to gather in for shelter.

"But they've burned us to the ground, son," interjected Mr. Monty.

In response, Isaiah leaped down to the grassy field, and all men followed his every movement with their eyes. "Look over there," Isaiah said, pointing to his ma and Miss Ferris's makeshift kitchen, where they handed out firsts and seconds of vegetable soup and corn bread to waiting townsfolk. "Do they look burned to you?"

A chorus of *no*s and even *no, sir*s followed Isaiah's moving, expressive body.

"What about there?" He motioned toward Mrs. Nichelle, who'd taken on the task of children under two. She'd gathered as many blankets as possible, stacking them onto the grass to create a playpen for the teetering bunch. "Does that look like a woman who's allowed her circumstance to stop her?"

Again, many *no*s and even more *no, sir*s rose from the small sphere of men. Vice Principal Anniston, Mrs. Nichelle's husband, waved over at her with such pride and gratitude that he had to wipe at his eyes.

"And then there's my Angel." Isaiah didn't make a show

of highlighting her; he instead looked at her calmly and with more reverence than he had toward anyone else in that field. "Savior. Teacher. Leader. There are not enough words to describe such a woman. She will never allow herself to be defeated by anyone, not even me. She is what our future looks like—brave and brilliant and still holding tight to the powerful forces that only come from one single source, love. She is Greenwood—riddled with heavy loss and pain but still moving onward. Upward. With resolve that no white man could ever regain. Once he's lost the likes of Angel, he's lost the lot of us.

"They will never have her, men, mark those words and brand them onto your arms and hearts and wills. She belongs, as much as she'd like, to me."

"Well, son," Mr. Morris called out. "Go to her."

Isaiah hopped from his stoop and walked briskly in Angel's direction. Her students oohed and aahed at his approach. Greenwood folks stopped and watched him closing the gap between himself and his love.

The closer he got, the more he picked up the pace. He wanted to lift her into the air. To breathe in her cocoa-butter skin as long as she'd allow him to. But when he was close enough to touch her, Truly stepped in front of him with her arms folded.

"May I help you, mister?"

Isaiah bent forward to meet Truly's large eyes. "I'd like to ask permission to speak with your teacher, if you please."

"You certainly may not," she said, tapping her foot in the dirt. "Just what are your intentions with Miss Angel? And tell the truth or I'll know."

After a quick wink in Isaiah's direction, Angel crouched in front of Truly.

"Truly, girl . . . ," she started. "The wisest man I've ever known once told me that mercy and truth can't exist without one another," Angel said, tucking a flyaway behind Truly's ear.

"Well," Truly replied, filled with attitude. "That's what I'm trying to do right now, Miss Angel. Get the truth out of this rambling boy called Isaiah Wilson."

"You should show mercy to Mr. Isaiah, correct?"

"How do I do that?" she asked.

"Allow him to pass."

As Truly, tiny but fierce, stepped aside, Isaiah pulled Angel in close and whispered, "Just so," into her ear.

Success is to be measured not so much by the position that one has reached in life as by the obstacles which he has overcome. —*Booker T. Washington*

I was born free. —*W.E.B. Du Bois*

My Author's Note Is an Acknowledgment

This novel began as my novels do—it was to be something else entirely. Before, it was the story of a fictional place I'd tentatively referred to as My Wakanda. No superheroes or fields of magical flowers to swallow, no. Just a simple, self-sustaining Black community where two Black teens got to freely fall in love. That's it. That's the magical place I was trying to write.

They rode bikes up and down flower-lined streets. They shared ice cream at the parlor owned by their neighbor named Fred. They went to the same pediatrician, Dr. Watts, on the corner in the squatty brick building just off Main Street. They loved books and movies and plain white milk straight from the carton. It was to be a quiet book where not much happened outside of the two of them going on about the business of falling in love.

I never expected that book to be published since there was no real story. I didn't care, though. I wrote it for me, dreaming more than I was writing. All the while visualizing a place where my Black daughter and Black son could walk and bike and eat ice cream and eventually fall in love in peace. That's Wakanda for me. Simplicity is My Wakanda. And writing it was a delight.

Greenwood after the attack, June 1921. (Getty Images)

But one afternoon in my wonderful friend Claudia Pearson's home, I met one of the best librarians in the world, Lisa Churchill. She asked me what I was working on, and I told her about the My Wakanda book. In response, she shared the story of Greenwood. My dream had been an actual place, realized in the 1900s. And then it was burned to the ground. Those two unnamed characters became Angel and Isaiah on the spot. And that sweet little novel became a complicated one, *Angel of Greenwood*.

As for acknowledgments, though . . .

I *acknowledge* that I am tired.

I *acknowledge* now that all I want from this life is a safe place for my Black children to get to fall in love.

I *acknowledge* that doesn't sound like a lot, but for Black folks in this country, it can be damn near impossible. And the burning of Greenwood and other places like it directly contributed to that near impossibility.

Greenwood today, never to be forgotten. (Top left: Associated Press; Top right: Associated Press; Bottom: Associated Press)

Finally, I *acknowledge* that so many Black people before me dreamed of their own versions of Wakanda, too.

Please allow me to *acknowledge* some of them:

Colonel Allen Allensworth	Allensworth, CA	1908
Oliver Toussaint Jackson	Dearfield, CO	1910
Joseph C. Clarke &		
Lewis Lawrence	Eatonville, FL	1887
Priscilla "Mother" Baltimore	Brooklyn, IL	1820s
Free Frank McWhorter	New Philadelphia, IL	1836
Joshua Lyles	Lyles Station, IN	1840s
Jack Moss	Mossville, LA	1790
Joe Penny	Pennytown, MO	1871
Isaiah Montgomery	Mound Bayou, MS	1887
Clem Deaver	DeWitty, NE	1907
Thomas Marshall	Marshalltown, NJ	1830s
Frank and Ella Boyer	Blackdom, NM	early 1900s
Frank and Ella Boyer	Vado, NM	1920s
Andrew Williams	Seneca Village, NY	1825
Epiphany Davis	Seneca Village, NY	1825
James Weeks	Weeksville, NY	1838
A. R. Brooks	Brooksville, OK	1903
Edward McCabe	Langston, OK	1890
E. L. Barber	Redbird, OK	1889
Harrison Barrett	Barrett, TX	1889
Jeff and Hanna Hill	Little Egypt, TX	1870
Anderson Moore	Moore Station, TX	1876
Robert and Dilsie Johnson	Mosier Valley, TX	1870s
James and Winnie Shankle	Shankleville, TX	1867

I sincerely hope someone writes books about them. EACH OF THEM DESERVES BOOKS! Do it, dammit! Or I will.

—Randi*

Facts of the Attack

While *Angel of Greenwood* is a fictional account, the 1921 Attack on the Greenwood District of Tulsa, Oklahoma, tragically happened.

After World War I, Greenwood was widely referred to first as the "Negro Wall Street of America" and later as the "Black Wall Street" because of their thriving business district and close-knit residential community. It was one of the most affluent Black communities in the country at the time, until the morning of May 30, 1921, in Tulsa's Drexel Building when a young white woman named Sarah Page screamed while riding an elevator with a young Black man named Dick Rowland.

What exactly happened on that elevator varies from person to person. Precisely what happened on that elevator may never be known. But as a result of Page's scream, Tulsa law enforcement officers arrested Dick Rowland the following day and began an investigation. That same day, an incendiary report in the *Tulsa Tribune* boasted the headline *Nab Negro for Attacking Girl in an Elevator*. This encouraged a confrontation at the courthouse where Rowland was being held. Several dozen Black men, some of them World War I veterans, armed themselves and went to the courthouse to protect Rowland from a threatening white mob gathering to attack him. Tempers flared, and shots were fired. Again, there are differing accounts of who shot first, but outnumbered, the Black people at the courthouse retreated back to the Greenwood District.

In the early morning hours of June 1, 1921, idyllic, prosperous, exceptional Greenwood was looted and burned by white rioters. In a span of fewer than twenty-four hours, thirty-five city blocks were charred, over eight hundred people were treated for injuries, and historians have estimated that somewhere between one hundred and three hundred lives were lost.

This event went largely unknown, even by descendants and residents of Tulsa. But in 2001, an official race riot commission named the Oklahoma Commission to Study the Tulsa Race Riot of 1921 was organized to review the details of the event. And recently, Tulsa Mayor G. T. Bynum launched an investigation into longstanding oral-history accounts of mass graves at various sites in Tulsa.

Inside of every Greenwood home burned that day in 1921 there was a story. Few who experienced it are alive today.

Many of those stories will never be told, though the Commission previously mentioned recorded interviews with many survivors still living at the time of its deliberations and report, some two decades ago. Angel and Isaiah are fictional. That much is true, but within them, I honor Greenwood. And, dear God, I pray I've done it justice.

Sources

1921 Tulsa Race Massacre Centennial Commission. tulsa2021.org.

Astor, Maggie. "What to Know About the Tulsa Greenwood Massacre." *The New York Times,* June 20, 2020. nytimes.com/2020/06/20/us/tulsa-greenwood-massacre.html.

Booker, Brakkton. "Excavation Begins for Possible Mass Grave From 1921 Tulsa Race Massacre." National Public Radio/WNYC, July 14, 2020. npr.org/sections/live-updates-protests-for-racial-justice/2020/07/14/890785747/excavation-begins-for-possible-mass-grave-from-1921-tulsa-race-massacre.

———. "Oklahoma Lawsuit Seeks Reparations in Connection to 1921 Tulsa Massacre." National Public Radio/WNYC, September 3, 2020. npr.org/sections/live-updates-protests-for-racial-justice/2020/09/03/909151983/oklahoma-lawsuit-seeks-reparations-in-connection-to-1921-tulsa-massacre.

Chakraborty, Ranjani. "The Massacre of Tulsa's 'Black Wall Street.'" *Vox,* February 27, 2019. youtube.com/watch?v=x-ItsPBTFO0.

Chang, Alisa. "The History and Legacy of Tulsa Race Massacre." *All Things Considered.* National Public Radio, June 19, 2020. npr.org/2020/06/19/880964037/the-history-and-legacy-of-tulsa-race-massacre.

Chang, Natalie. "The Massacre of Black Wall Street." TheAtlantic.com, sponsored by *Watchmen* on HBO. theatlantic.com/sponsored/hbo-2019/the-massacre-of-black-wall-street/3217/?gclid=CjwKCAjwzvX7BRAeEiwAsXExo3hJzVqPLs0tewzrNk5fXZ4S46YW3WxXetPRoYjYxWJRmFudYzcopBoCu34QAvD_BwE.

Clark, Alexis. "Tulsa's Black Wall Street Flourished as a Self-Contained Hub in the Early 1900s." History.com, January 2, 2020. history.com/news/black-wall-street-tulsa-race-massacre.

Clark, Nia. "Introduction: Black Wall Street 1921." *Black Wall Street 1921*, January 29, 2020. blackwallstreet-1921.com.

Editors of *Encyclopedia Britannica* online. "Tulsa Race Massacre of 1921." *Encyclopedia Britannica* online, September 30, 2020. britannica.com/event/Tulsa-race-riot-of-1921.

Editors of *Tulsa World*. "Read an Early Tulsa World Account of the Tulsa Race Riot." *Tulsa World*, May 30, 2016. tulsaworld.com /news/local/june-1-1921-read-an-early-tulsa-world-account -of-the-tulsa-race-riot/article_569a56c8-93f8-502c-b236 -ac91aa632e51.html.

Ellsworth, Scott. "Tulsa Race Massacre." Oklahoma Historical Society. okhistory.org/publications/enc/entry .php?entry=TU013.

Frazee, Gretchen. "What Happened 99 Years Ago in the Tulsa Race Massacre." *PBS News Hour*, June 19, 2020. pbs.org/newshour /nation/what-happened-99-years-ago-in-the-tulsa-race-massacre.

Huddleston, Tom, Jr. "'Black Wall Street': The history of the wealthy Black community and the massacre perpetrated there." CNBC .com, July 4, 2020. cnbc.com/2020/07/04/what-is-black-wall -street-history-of-the-community-and-its-massacre.html.

Johnson, Hannibal B. *Acres of Aspiration: The All-Black Towns of Oklahoma.* Fort Worth, Texas: Eakin Press, 2002.

———. *Black Wall Street: From Riot to Renaissance in Tulsa's Historic Greenwood District.* Fort Worth, Texas: Eakin Press, 2007.

———. *Black Wall Street 100: An American City Grapples with Its Historical Rachial Trauma.* Fort Worth, Texas: Eakin Press, 2020.

———. *Tulsa's Historic Greenwood District.* Mount Pleasant, South Carolina: Arcadia Publishing, 2014.

Keyes, Allison. "A Long-Lost Manuscript Contains a Searing Eyewitness Account of the Tulsa Race Massacre of 1921." *Smithsonian Magazine*, May 27, 2016. smithsonianmag.com

/smithsonian-institution/long-lost-manuscript-contains-searing
-eyewitness-account-tulsa-race-massacre-1921-180959251.

Madigan, Tim. *The Burning: Massacre, Destruction, and the Tulsa Race
Riot of 1921*. New York: St. Martins Griffin, 2003.

Merrefield, Clark. "The 1921 Tulsa Race Massacre and the Financial
Fallout." *The Harvard Gazette*, June 18, 2020. news.harvard.edu
/gazette/story/2020/06/the-1921-tulsa-race-massacre-and-its
-enduring-financial-fallout.

Parrish, Mary E. Jones. *Events of the Tulsa Disaster*. January 1, 1923.
Out of print; limited edition available via John Hope Franklin
Center for Reconciliation.

Reporters of *The Morning Tulsa Daily World*. "Barrett Commends
Tulsa for Co-operaton With the State Military Authorities." *The
Morning Tulsa Daily World*, June 4, 1921. chroniclingamerica.loc
.gov/lccn/sn85042345/1921-06-04/ed-1/seq-2.

Rivenes, Erik. "The 1921 Tulsa Race Massacre w/Tim Madigan."
Most Notorious. podcasts.apple.com/au/podcast/1921
-tulsa-race-massacre-w-tim-madigan-true-crime-history
/id1055044256?i=1000477017630.

Romo, Vanessa. "New Research Identifies Possible Mass Graves
from 1921 Tulsa Race Massacre." National Public Radio/WNYC,
December 17, 2019. npr.org/2019/12/17/789015343/new
-research-identifies-possible-mass-graves-from1921-tulsa-race
-massacre.

Tulsa Historical Society and Museum. "1921 Tulsa Race Massacre."
Exhibit, Tulsa, Oklahoma. tulsahistory.org/exhibit/1921-tulsa
-race-massacre.

Wondery. "Tulsa Race Massacres, Episodes 2019." *American History
Tellers*, May 29, 2019. stitcher.com/podcast/wondery/american
-history-tellers/e/61379087.

Young, Nicole, producer. "Exhume the Truth." *60 Minutes*, June 14,
2020. youtube.com/watch?v=yA8t8PW-OkA.

THANK YOU FOR READING THIS FEIWEL & FRIENDS BOOK.
THE FRIENDS WHO MADE

ANGEL OF GREENWOOD

POSSIBLE ARE:

JEAN FEIWEL, PUBLISHER

LIZ SZABLA, ASSOCIATE PUBLISHER

RICH DEAS, SENIOR CREATIVE DIRECTOR

HOLLY WEST, SENIOR EDITOR

ANNA ROBERTO, SENIOR EDITOR

KAT BRZOZOWSKI, SENIOR EDITOR

DAWN RYAN, SENIOR MANAGING EDITOR

KIM WAYMER, SENIOR PRODUCTION MANAGER

ERIN SIU, ASSOCIATE EDITOR

EMILY SETTLE, ASSOCIATE EDITOR

RACHEL DIEBEL, ASSISTANT EDITOR

FOYINSI ADEGBONMIRE, EDITORIAL ASSISTANT

FOLLOW US ON FACEBOOK OR
VISIT US ONLINE AT FIERCEREADS.COM.

OUR BOOKS ARE FRIENDS FOR LIFE.